D0588878
Ticket to
Heaven

Also by *Vivien Alcock*

The Cuckoo Sister
The Face at the Window
Ghostly Companions
The Haunting of Cassie Palmer
A Kind of Thief
The Monster Garden
Singer to the Sea God
The Stonewalkers
The Sylvia Game
The Trial of Anna Cotman

for younger readers

Gift on a String
Othergran

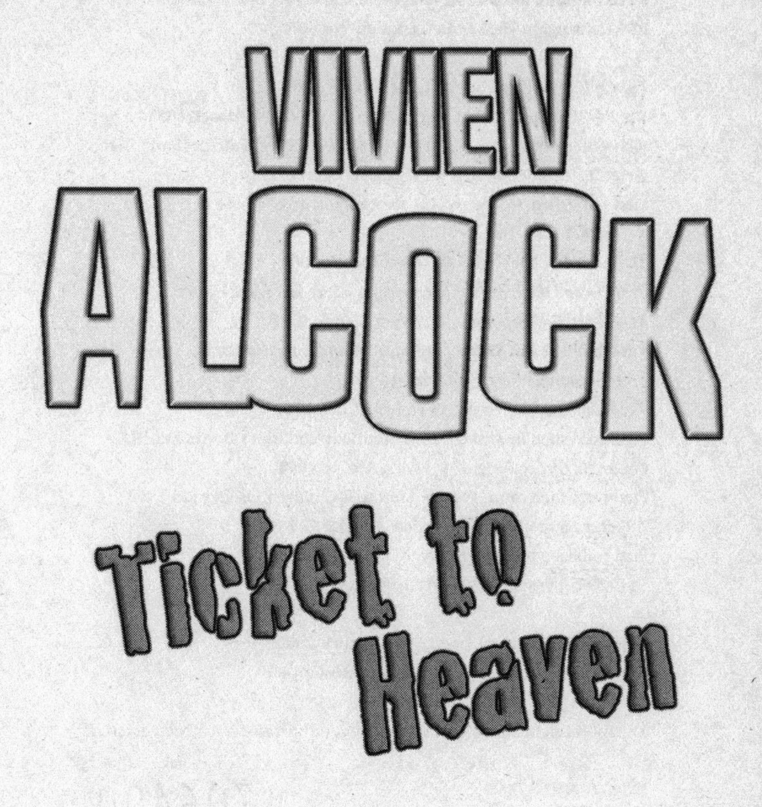
VIVIEN
ALCOCK
Ticket to
Heaven

Mammoth

First published in Great Britain 2000
by Mammoth, an imprint of Egmont Children's Books Limited
239 Kensington High Street, London W8 6SA

ISBN 0 7497 3786 7

10 9 8 7 6 5 4 3 2 1

A CIP catalogue record for this title
is available from the British Library

Printed in Great Britain
by Cox & Wyman Ltd, Reading, Berkshire

Contents

The Crab Boy 1

The Boy who Swallowed a Ghost 13

Ticket to Heaven 31

The Paper-boy 46

Orpheus and the Underworld 62

Second-best Boy 79

The Pram Lady 94

Cinderella Girl 108

A Proper Boy 120

Sad Ada 139

The Crab Boy

When Tim was a baby, his uncle Robert dropped him into the sea. On purpose. Not that he meant to drown him, no indeed! Uncle Robert was a kind man. But he was not very sensible. To be honest, although an excellent person in many ways, he was exceedingly silly. He believed everything he was told.

It happened like this. Uncle Robert sat next to a man on the bus who told him that boys were born knowing how to swim. Like fish or dogs. The secret was to catch them young, before they'd learned to be afraid.

'Just drop them in deep water,' the man had said, 'and hey presto, away they'll go. No trouble at all. Fish, dogs, tadpoles, boys, they're all the same.'

Anyone but Uncle Robert would have noticed that the man was tipsy. There was a white carnation in his buttonhole, a haze of champagne round his head, and he was waving his pink hands around as if conducting the wedding march. No one but Uncle Robert would have believed a word he said. Unluckily for poor Tim, Uncle Robert always believed everything he was told.

The next day, when Mrs Jenkins took her two little daughters and her baby son down to the beach, Uncle Robert came too. He gave the little girls an ice cream each, kissed his sister and then bent over the carrycot.

'Would you like to go for a swim?' he whispered.

Tim had not yet learned to say 'no'. He lay there, smiling and burping and bubbling, not guessing for a moment the terrible thing that was about to happen to him.

His uncle picked him out of the carrycot and carried him across the beach.

Mrs Jenkins was making a sandcastle for the girls and did not notice until too late. Uncle Robert walked into the sea. On and on he went, inch by chilly inch, until it was up to his waist. Then he stopped. Tim, high on his shoulders, crowed with delight. He didn't know his uncle was given to silly ideas. Nobody had told him. It came as a terrible shock.

Down and down Tim sank into the cold dim wetness, leaving a string of screaming bubbles behind him. Bitter water rushed into his open mouth and up his nose and flooded his eyes with the salt tears of the sea. Down he dropped like a stone right to the sandy bottom. He thought it was the end of his warm milky world, and his heart nearly burst with grief.

Uncle Robert bent down and scooped the choking baby up. He held him upside down and patted the water out of him. Then he handed him back to his mother who had come rushing down to the water's edge.

'As good as new,' he said, looking nervous, as well he might.

Mrs Jenkins held Tim tight in her arms and wept. 'You nearly killed him! My poor little baby, you've nearly drowned him. You're a fool! I'll never forgive you.'

But she did. People always forgave Uncle Robert because he was so sorry when his ideas went wrong, as they often did. He would come round with his arms full of flowers and his pockets bulging with presents for the children. The best present was always for Tim.

'It's not because he likes you best,' his sister Mary told him, 'it's only because he nearly drowned you once.'

Tim could not remember being dropped into the sea, though his sisters had told him about it. But now Mary said, 'It wasn't really Uncle Robert. Mum just says that because she doesn't want to frighten you. It was the crab boy. When you were a baby, he nearly got you.'

'What crab boy? What do you mean?'

'Don't tell him,' Liz said, 'he'll only have nightmares and wake up screaming, and Mum will blame us.'

But when Liz went off to her piano lesson, Tim begged Mary to tell him, and she did. She didn't think it was fair that he always got the best presents. Besides, she rather liked frightening people.

'He's a ghost,' she said, rolling her eyes. 'The crab boy catches people by the heels and pulls them down into the sea. He nearly drowned you once. I bet he was mad that you got away.'

'Why did he pick on me?' Tim asked. 'Who was he?'

'Just a boy. About your age now. He lived with his widowed mother in one of these cottages. Might have been this very one, but it was so long ago, no one remembers exactly. They were very poor. He used to go looking for crabs for their supper. One night he never came back. They say a man stole his crabs and pushed him into the water, and so he wants revenge.' Liz glanced slyly at Tim and put on her older sister's voice. 'He made his living out of the sea. But he never learned to swim, so he made his dying out of it too. Don't you think that was silly of him?'

Tim scowled. She was getting at him again. He still could not swim. His mother, his sisters and Uncle Robert had all offered to teach him.

'No!' Tim always said, his face going as white as chalk, 'I can't! I won't! I feel sick! Mum, don't make me.'

His mother sighed. 'If only your uncle Robert hadn't dropped you into the sea when you were a baby,' she said. And she'd given him a note to take to school, asking for him to be excused swimming lessons.

It hadn't mattered when he was small. Many of his friends couldn't swim then. They played games on the beach. They ran through the shallow frills of the sea, kicking up water with their feet. They built great fortresses of sand, complete with moats and drawbridges, and turrets decorated with pebbles and flags of seaweed.

But one by one, Tim's friends learned to swim and left him. Until at last he stood on the sand, surrounded by little kids half his age. Far out, he saw the heads of his friends bobbing like Hallowe'en apples in the deep water.

'Come on in!' they shouted. 'It's great! It's not a bit cold!'

'I can't!' he shouted back. 'I'm not allowed to swim. I've got a weak chest.'

'That's a good excuse,' somebody said.

He turned round. Nell Jones from his school was standing behind him, her dark hair blowing in the wind.

'It's true,' he told her. 'Whenever I go into water up to my knees, my heart rattles about in my chest like it's going to come loose.'

'So does mine,' she said.

'Does it?' he asked, pleased to find somebody who knew what it was like. 'And I can't breathe properly.'

'Nor can I.'

'And then I feel faint, and the sea roars in my ears like a lion.'

'Mine sounds more like a tiger,' she said, smiling.

'You must have a weak chest like me,' he told her, thinking she'd be pleased to have a good excuse too.

But to his surprise, she laughed and said, 'That's not what my dad calls it. My dad says it's sea-fright. Funk. He calls me his scaredy-cat. I'm glad you are scared too.'

'I'm not!' he protested. 'It's my chest, my weak chest. I've had it ever since I was a baby. Everybody knows –'

'Everybody knows you're scared of the crab boy,' she said.

'You're stupid,' he said, and walked away.

She shrieked after him, dancing wildly on the wet sand,

> 'Tim! Tim! Won't swim
> For fear the crab boy catches him!'

And all the little kids looked up from their sandcastles and stared at him as he walked by.

He would never go down to the beach again. He hated

the sea. He wished it would evaporate. Why hadn't he been born in the middle of a desert.

It was a hot summer. Every day his friends went down to the sea to swim and Tim walked by himself in the dusty streets. The shop windows were full of toy boats and shell boxes, rubber rings and fishing nets. Then he walked over the dry hills behind the town. The sheep raised their heads to watch him pass, but nobody called him a coward. Nobody spoke to him at all. He was very lonely.

One day, he met his uncle Robert striding over the hills.

'Hullo, Tim, all alone? Where are your friends?' he asked.

'They've gone swimming,' Tim said.

Uncle Robert looked guilty, as well he might. 'If only I hadn't dropped you into the sea when you were a baby,' he sighed. 'What can we do about it? Let's sit on the grass and think.'

They sat down, side by side. While his uncle thought, Tim plucked at the grass with his fingers and made a little haystack. When it was two inches high, Uncle Robert said, 'I've got an idea. I met an old fisherman on the bus the other day, and he told me that every year, before taking his boat out, he used to throw a coin into the sea.'

'Why?'

'To pay for what he was about to take out of it. Well, I snatched you out of the sea when you were a baby, and I never paid for you. Perhaps that brought us bad luck. Come on.'

Uncle Robert sprang to his feet and held out his hand to Tim. They went running down the hill towards the town and the sea. Once on the beach, they stood side by side at the water's edge. Uncle Robert put his hand in his picket and drew out a handful of coins; pennies and pounds and ten pence pieces. Tim watched, wondering how much his uncle would decide he was worth.

'You're worth more than money,' his uncle said kindly, 'but it's only a token payment. A silvery coin for the silvery sea.'

He picked out a ten pence piece and threw it far out into the water. Before they moved away, a little brown dog came swimming out of the sea with a piece of driftwood in its mouth. It dropped it on the sand at their feet and ran off. They looked down. In a crack in the wood was wedged a ten pence piece.

'The sea's given it back,' Tim said, his face as white as foam, 'it's out to get me.'

His uncle wanted to throw the coin in again, wanted to throw in all the money in his pockets and his wallet too, but Tim wouldn't let him.

'Let me keep this ten pence, Uncle Robert,' he said, 'I want to try an idea of my own.'

That evening after his tea, Tim went down to the beach by himself. The tide was out and the wet sand was wrinkled like fingers that have been in the water too long. There was nobody about. Tim took off his shoes and left them by the sea wall. Then he crossed the sand to where the rocks stretched out to the distant sea.

He picked his way across them carefully. Many were slippery with weed that hung down like mermaid's hair into the shadowed pools. When he reached a flat rock that jutted out into the sea, he stopped and looked round. There was no one in sight. He turned back to the sea.

'Crab boy! Crab boy!' he shouted. 'It wasn't me who stole your crabs. I wasn't even born when it happened. I'm not a man. I'm only a boy, like you.'

His voice bounced over the still water like a thrown pebble, 'You . . . you . . . you.'

'I'm your friend,' Tim cried. 'Look, I've brought you a present!'

He tossed the ten pence coin into the sea, and watched it twisting down out of sight. No hand reached out from behind the curtain of water to catch it as it fell.

How stupid of me, he thought, what a waste of money.

The sun had gone in and a cold wind was blowing. He heard an odd noise behind him, a faint scraping, pattering sound. He turned.

The rock was alive with crabs, crawling with them; crabs as large as apple pies, crabs as small as shirt buttons. Some were pinky brown, some dirty green, some mottled grey. One large one wore a barnacle on its back like a party hat. And all of them were looking at him with their tiny eyes.

'Go away!' Tim shouted, frightened.

A small yellow crab with long spidery legs ran sideways over the craggy backs of its neighbours. A dusty one, with fierce red eyes, reared up on its back legs and waved inky claws at him.

The sea was behind him. There was no way to go but forwards. He took a step towards them, but his bare foot on the grey rock looked as pink and tender as ham. He snatched it back again.

The crabs began shuffling sideways, some to the right, some to the left, in the pattern of a weird dance. Though they never moved directly towards him, he noticed they were edging a little nearer. And nearer. Forcing him backwards towards the sea.

'Help me!' he cried – and heard a rush and tinkle as something came out of the water. He turned.

A naked boy stood dripping on the rock. A thin boy,

smaller than he was. His wet hair was as brown as tangle-weed and his skin as pale as bone. His eyes were greenish and bulged a little, like bubbles in old glass.

'Is this for me?' he asked, and held out his hand to show the ten pence coin.

Tim was so frightened that he could only nod his head.

'I can't eat it,' the boy said, 'and I can't spend it. Still, thank you kindly. I'll take it from you.'

Then he smiled very sweetly, reached out his ice-cold hand and pushed Tim into the sea.

Down and down Tim sank into the cold, dim wetness, just as he had done when he was a baby. Only this time there was no Uncle Robert to scoop him out of the sea.

His feet touched the bottom and he kicked himself upwards. His head burst out into the open air, gasping and spluttering. Through his wet eyes he had a glimmering vision of the boy dancing on the rock, with the crabs lurching around him, clicking their claws like castanets. Above the roar of the sea in his ears, he thought he heard a voice shrieking, 'Swim! Swim if you can, you mutt! Or sink. It's all the same to me.'

Tim began pawing the water like a dog, and suddenly he was swimming towards the rock, his chin in the air. He opened his mouth to shout in triumph but a wave splashed into it, and his head went under the water.

When he stood up, he found the sea was only up to his chest and the rock was within reach of his hand. The boy and the crabs were gone.

The next day, Tim went down to the beach early. He saw Nell Jones walking on the sands by herself.

'Watch me,' he said, and running into the sea, he began to swim.

She stood and watched him, her long black hair blowing in the wind. When he came out, she said sadly, 'Now I'll be the only one left who can't swim.'

'I'll teach you,' he said, 'for a ten pence piece.'

She thought about it. 'You won't duck me or play nasty tricks?'

'No. Cross my heart,' he said, and put his hand to his chest where the crab boy's icy fingers had touched him.

'All right,' she agreed, 'when?'

'Come with me now,' he said, and smiled very sweetly. Then he pinched her arm gently between his fingers and moved off towards the sea. Sideways, like a crab.

The Boy who Swallowed a Ghost

His name was John Dafte, or as the school register put it, Dafte John. No one made jokes about it. He was a tall, hairy boy, with huge shoulders and long arms and a voice like a big drum. Junior boxing champion, captain of both the cricket and football teams – there wasn't a sport he didn't excel at. We called him, respectfully, Prince Kong.

I admired him tremendously. He was a smiling, good-natured hero, with a strong sense of fair play. He had only to stroll out into the playground for the bullies to crawl back into their holes.

'Pick on someone your own size,' he'd say. (It must have limited *his* choice: there was no one at school anywhere near his size. He dwarfed even the masters.) I thought him a true prince. It didn't worry me that he looked like a gorilla. I *like* gorillas.

One the Monday morning after half-term, he came to school with two black eyes, and a split and swollen nose, decorated with dark scabs like beetles.

We crowded round him sympathetically.

'Hey, Prince, you got dark glasses on?'

''Ad an argument with a bulldozer, 'ave you?'

'Your mum been beating you up?'

I was not as surprised as the others that he should have come off worst in a fight. I'm good at maths, and can work out that it's no use having the strength of ten, if you happen to pick a quarrel with eleven. It would be just like Prince Kong, I thought, to go charging in to save someone from a gang of toughs, without stopping to count. What did puzzle me was that he should lie about it. I'd have expected him to smile and say, 'Can't win 'em all.' Something like that.

Instead he shouldered us roughly out of his way, his head down, his eyes furtive, muttering furiously, 'Walked into a door.'

'Poor old door, it didn't stand a chance,' I said, and wished I hadn't when he glared at me. 'Sorry, Prince,' I said hastily, stepping back. I am thin and, like glass, very breakable.

We watched him limp into the school building, and followed at a safe distance, puzzled and a little dismayed.

He and I were in different forms, so I did not see him again until school was over. I was waiting for one of my friends when he came down the steps, caught sight of me and hesitated, staring at me out of his bruised eyes. For the first time I felt nervous of him, and smiled uneasily. He limped over and stood looking down at me. A long way down.

'You're clever, aren't you?' he said.

I thought he was referring to my stupid remark about the door, and said hastily, 'I'm sorry, Prince. I didn't mean . . . I was only joking.'

'What?' he asked, puzzled, then shrugged the question away and went on, 'I mean, you come top all the time. Brainy. Good at working things out – you know, problems.'

I wriggled my shoulders and replied with regulation modesty, 'Oh, I dunno. Just lucky, I guess.'

'No. You're clever,' he repeated. I realised suddenly that he wanted me to be clever. His eyes, between their swollen, discoloured lids, were gazing at me pleadingly. If it had been anyone else but Prince Kong, I'd have thought he was frightened.

'Well . . .' I said – it wasn't the thing to boast, but I didn't want to let him down – 'sort of, I suppose.'

I thought he looked relieved but he did not say anything. The silence became embarrassing.

'Is there . . .? Can I . . .? I mean, if there's anything I can do, just ask,' I mumbled, uneasy beneath his strange, gloomy stare. 'Is it maths? Latin? Not that I'm all that good . . .' I tailed off.

'Walking home with anybody?' he asked.

'No,' I lied. I could see Mark on the steps, watching us from a respectful distance. I knew he would understand. It was an honour to walk with Prince Kong. Anyone would have jumped at the chance.

'Can I come with you, then?' he asked. 'Only I got a problem, see?'

'Yes,' I said eagerly, 'of course.' I didn't see. I couldn't imagine what problem it could be. Not maths or Latin. Prince Kong never worried about his school work. Conscious of his own enormous power, he was content to stay at the bottom, like a submarine lying low.

'If you tell anybody, I'll skin you,' he said.

'I won't!'

'You'd better not.'

* * *

I don't live far enough from the school. Ten minutes later, we were standing outside my home, and still he hadn't told me what it was all about. I don't think he distrusted me. I honestly think he just could not get the words out. He kept turning towards me, opening and shutting his mouth like a giant fish, with nothing coming out but air and a faint smell of onions.

'What's the problem, then?' I asked at last.

But this direct approach seemed to alarm him.

'I dunno,' he mumbled.

We stood in the afternoon sunlight and looked at each other hopelessly.

'Come in and have a Coke?' I suggested.

He hesitated. 'Don't feel like meeting nobody,' he said. 'Not like this.' He gestured towards his bruised face.

I reassured him that my mother and father were both at work. Wouldn't be back till gone six. I took him indoors, settled him into a chair in our kitchen and poured him a large Coke. Then I sat opposite him, and waited.

He shifted uneasily. 'It's . . .' he began, with that strange frightened look in his eyes. 'It's . . .' He paused. I could almost hear the levers creaking in his head as he changed lines. 'It's me maths,' he finished, looking at me fiercely, challenging me to call him a liar. 'Can't make it out.' He plonked a book on the table, opening it at random. 'All that,' he said, waving a large hand, 'don't mean a thing.'

I was disappointed. I knew he didn't really care a fig for his maths. But no one in their right minds would argue with Prince Kong, so I picked up the book and began to explain it to him. His eyes glazed. His mouth fell open and he sighed. I didn't think he was listening. I bent my head over the book . . .

Suddenly I heard the noise of his chair scraping on the tiled floor. I looked up and saw he had got to his feet. He looked . . . different. There was a grim, determined look on his face. As I watched, he walked across the kitchen. Quickly. Firmly. With the air of someone who knew where he was going. Walked with his eyes open, slap bang into the wall! His damaged nose hit the painted plaster with a squelchy smack, leaving a smear of blood like jam.

'Prince!' I cried in amazement.

He staggered back, his hands to his bleeding face. I guided him to his chair and gave him a clean tea towel soaked in cold water. He pressed it to his nose. Above it, his eyes looked at me miserably, full of fear.

'Shall I ring the doctor?' I asked.

He shook his head.

'Is it your eyes?' I thought perhaps he was suffering from some kind of intermittent blindness. But he shook his head again.

'What is it? What's the matter?'

He took the tea towel from his face. It was patched with his blood. His nose was dark red and I could almost see it swelling before my eyes.

'Prince, what's the matter?' I asked again.

'You'll laugh.'

'I won't!' I protested, astonished he should think me so heartless.

It was then, at last, that he managed to get the words out.

'I think I've swallowed a ghost.'

I stared at him.

'*What*?'

'Ghost,' he repeated firmly 'G.H.O.S.T. Spirit. Spook.'

'Oh.'

He looked at me suspiciously. A spasm of suppressed laughter was shaking me. I couldn't help it. It was partly nerves, I think. I shut my mouth firmly and tried to make my face show nothing but sympathetic inquiry.

'It wouldn't have happened,' he said gloomily, 'if I'd kept my mouth shut.'

He told me he had been staying with his aunt and uncle in Bell Green during the holiday. One night, after supper, they'd got to talking about ghosts. You know the way it is, he said. Everybody knows someone who's seen one. His aunt had told them there was a ghost in Bell

Green. She hadn't seen it herself, but lots of people had. When the moon was full, it came out of the river, white as mist, and drifted over the fields at night, howling . . .

'Sheila, that's me cousin, she laughed and said she'd bet that's all it was. Mist and wind and moonlight. But Auntie wouldn't have it. For one thing, she said it always come up at the same spot. By the bridge near the old timber mill. A man had drowned himself there once, years ago . . . "Most like fell in when he was drunk," I said, teasing her. She got quite cross. "Why don't you go and see for yourselves," me uncle said, winking at me, "it's a nice night for a walk."'

So they had gone out, Prince Kong and his cousin Sheila, strolling along the river bank in the moonlight.

'Dunno that we was bothering about the old ghost much,' he said with a sly smile, 'but then we come to this bridge, and there was the old mill facing us on a bend in the river. "This must be the place," Sheila said, and we leaned on the parapet and looked down. Couldn't make out nothing at first. Just sort of splinters of the moon in the water, and reeds, stiff and black like railings. Then we saw it. A bit of mist, thin as string, rising out of the river. Like a white worm it was, wriggling and squirming. Higher and higher it come till it was level with our faces, no more than a foot away. Then it sort of ballooned out into a face. A man's face. I saw it with me own eyes! Not clear – more like when you've caught a right hook on your chin and you see things a bit hazy. Sheila grabbed hold of me arm, and I . . . well, I sort of drew me breath in sharpish . . . and *swallowed him*! Are you laughing?' he demanded angrily.

'No,' I said quickly. 'Go on.'

'He'd thinned out again, see, and he slipped down me throat like spaghetti. I could feel him all the way down. Cold. Like ice. It was horrible.'

'What did you do?'

'Well, I tried to cough him up, but he wouldn't come. Soon as I got back to Auntie's, I went to the bathroom, and stuck me finger down me throat. Sicked up all me supper down the bog. Waste of good food. It didn't do no good. Frightened him, though,' he said with grim satisfaction. 'I could feel him scuttling about inside like an ice cube on the run. Banging into me ribs, freezing me heart . . . He's up here now,' he said, tapping his head. He gave the ghost of a smile. 'Plenty of room at the top. I'm not brainy like you.'

'Does it hurt?' I asked curiously.

'Not hurt, exactly. It's just cold. Terribly cold.' He put his huge red hand on his head as if to warm it. 'It's numbing me brain. I wouldn't mind so much if the silly beggar didn't think he could still walk through walls and closed doors. Look at me face! That's our kitchen shelf. That's our front door,' he said, pointing to the various bruises on his face, 'that's a brick wall. And he's done me nose five times. Six, counting your wall. Yesterday he walked me into a 210 bus. Luckily I wasn't killed. I dunno what to do. Every time me mind goes blank, he does something daft. It's got me beat.'

I no longer felt like laughing. Prince sat there, his great head bowed, his strong hands helpless on the table.

'You mustn't let your mind go blank, Prince,' I said. 'You must keep thinking all the time . . .'

'All the time?' he repeated, looking at me with amazement.

'Yes.'

He shook his head. 'Couldn't do it, Mike,' he said decidedly. 'Not all the time. Out of practice, see? More used to thinking with me hands and feet. Got a clever body, Dad says. After all,' he added defensively, 'we can't all have brains in the same place. No reason why they got to be in the head, is there?'

'Well,' I said, 'it's more usual.'

'Anyway, what about when I go to sleep? Can't go without sleep for ever. Got you there!'

I had to admit it. We sat there, trying to think. I was supposed to be clever, but I have to confess I hadn't an idea in my head. It was Prince Kong who thought of something first.

'Hit me,' he said suddenly.

'Hit you?'

'Yeah. Here,' he jutted out his granite chin. 'Might jolt him out, see?'

I hesitated.

'Come on. Hit me.'

I clenched my fist. It looked as small and as fragile as a glass bead. We both looked at it dubiously. Prince shook his head.

'Got small hands, haven't you? I reckon the wall hit me harder than you could. Pity. Don't want to bust your knuckles for nothing.'

'Sorry.'

'Not your fault,' he said kindly.

We sat silently again, racking our brains.

'This man, why did he drown himself?' I asked.

'Dunno. Auntie didn't say. Don't matter, does it?'

'I thought it might help if we knew something about him.'

Prince brightened. 'Yeah. Study his form. Find out whether he favours the right or the left . . .' He looked despondent again. 'Don't see how it helps with a ghost, though.'

'Does he walk every night?'

'No. Full moon, Auntie said.'

'I wonder where he is the rest of the time?'

'Dunno. Back in the river, I suppose.'

The river . . .

'Bell Green is in Hertfordshire, isn't it?' I asked.

'Yeah.'

'North of here?'

'Yeah.'

I pointed to the smear of blood on the wall. 'That's north,' I said.

Prince looked puzzled. 'What are you getting at?'

'Perhaps he's trying to get back to the river. Perhaps he just wants to go home. Look, let's go there – it's not far, is it? You could open your mouth over the water and let him out. It's worth trying.'

He looked at me admiringly. 'I said you was clever, Mike.'

I beamed. I really thought I was clever. You see, I didn't really believe in the ghost. I'd stopped believing in ghosts when I was six. I thought it was all in his imagination. Perhaps in his last fight, he'd been hit too hard on his head and was still a bit punch drunk. That, and the moonlight and the mist. All I had to do, I thought, was convince him I'd seen the ghost come out of his mouth and plop into the river . . . must get him to shut his eyes . . . throw a stone into the water to make a splash . . .

'Trust me, Prince,' I said smugly. Fool that I was.

It was only half past five. I left a note for my mother

saying I was going to supper with a friend, and would be back latish. We took the tube to Barnet, and then caught a bus to Bell Green.

The light was fading when we came to the bridge, and the river looked cold and dirty. Tall nettles grew up the banks.

'Shall we go right down to the water?' Prince asked.

I looked at the nettles.

'No. Just as good from here. Can you still feel him?'

He nodded and tapped his head. 'Here,' he said.

'Lean over the bridge and shut your eyes,' I instructed.

'Shut me eyes? Why?'

'Er . . . to help your mind go blank,' I improvised. 'You said that's when he did things.'

Obligingly Prince leaned over the parapet, his head hanging down, his mouth open, eyes shut. I bent down and picked up a small stone. But before I could toss it into the water, he groaned suddenly and straightened up.

'What's the matter?' I asked.

'Oh my God, oh my God!' he cried, with terrible anguish, and turned his face towards me. I backed away, staring. His face was moving, twitching, jerking, as if a battle was taking place beneath the skin.

'Prince!' I shouted, terrified. 'Prince!'

'Oh my God!' he said again, and his voice was utterly different, unfamiliar.

'John!' I cried, using his real name for the first time, 'John Dafte! *Come back*!'

For a moment I thought I saw the boy I knew looking out of the bruised eyes. Then his face changed again.

'God help me,' the ghost groaned. Blundering past me, he left the bridge, stumbled down through the nettles to the water's edge and threw himself in.

I ran after him, slipping on the steep bank, stinging my hands. He was thrashing about in the water, his fists flailing as if he were fighting himself.

'Prince! Prince, you can swim! You're the champion, remember?' I shouted. I slipped off my shoes and was tearing off my anorak and trousers. 'Swim, Prince! Swim to the bank!'

I don't know if he heard me. He put his arms above his head and disappeared.

I dived in. The water was so cold. And dark. I could not see him. I swam desperately backwards and forwards, feeling about with my hands. Once I thought I had hold of his hair and pulled, but it was only weeds.

'Please, God, let me find him!' I prayed.

Suddenly his huge figure rose up in front of me, face pale in the dim light, wild eyes staring. I swam up to him, but he lashed out with his arm and knocked me away in a boil of bubbles. Then he was gone again.

I dived into the spreading circle of ripples, spreading my arms under the water. My hand caught hold of cloth, an arm . . . I pulled. He did not fight me this time. He could not. I towed him to the river's edge and slid his heavy body on to a patch of mud and reeds. I could not lift him on to the bank.

He was not breathing.

I turned his head to one side, and pulled his slimy tongue forward, trying desperately to remember what I knew about the kiss of life. Then I put my mouth over his, and breathed as hard as I could. His lips tasted of mud and foul water, and were horribly cold. In and out, I breathed into his massive lungs, in and out, in and out. I was crying, my tears falling on his wet face. In and out, in and out.

He's dead, I thought. I've killed him.

Then suddenly his chest heaved. He breathed in, emptying my lungs till I felt like a vacuum flask. Then he breathed out again, air and water, cold as ice. Now he was coughing and choking, spitting out great mouthfuls of the river on to the mud and reeds, while I thumped him on the back, laughing and crying, happier than I had ever been before.

An hour later, we were sitting in borrowed pyjamas, wrapped in blankets, by his aunt's gas fire in Bell Green. A passing truck and two strong farmers had heard my shouts and come to our rescue.

'Your mum and dad are coming right over, Mike,' she told me. She put her hand on my forehead, and frowned. 'You're shivering, yet you feel hot. I hope you haven't caught a chill. Funny, it was our Johnny that near drowned, yet he's almost got over it. While you . . .'

'I'm all right,' I said.

'I'm going to make a bed up for you,' she decided. 'I don't think you're fit to go home tonight. I don't like the look of you at all.' She smiled, and kissed the top of my head. 'You saved our Johnny's life,' she said. 'We got to take good care of you.'

When she had left the room, Prince Kong looked at me anxiously.

'You bad?' he asked.

'No.'

'Want the fire up higher?'

'No. I'm hot.'

'You're shivering.'

'I know.'

'You haven't caught something, have you?'

'Yes!' I shouted unhappily. 'I've caught your blinking ghost!'

There was a pause. Then he said slowly, 'You gave me the kiss of life, didn't you?'

I nodded.

'And that's when . . .?'

'When you breathed out,' I said. 'I had my mouth open.'

He frowned. 'Where is he?' he said fiercely.

I put my hand on my head. 'Here.'

'Like a cube of ice?'

'Yes.'

'Sort of numbing your brain?'

'Yes.' My voice shook. 'I'll never get my GCSEs now,' I said miserably.

Another silence. Then Prince got to his feet.

'Stand up, Mike,' he said, with so much authority in his voice that I stood up immediately, looking at him in bewilderment.

'Sorry, mate,' he said. I saw it coming; a huge fist shooting towards me. My head exploded. Everything went red. Green. Black.

Well, here I am, a hero, in hospital with a broken jaw. Everyone makes a fuss of me. Prince Kong came to visit me this afternoon, tiptoeing over the polished floor of the ward, a pile of comics under his arm.

He sat down on the chair by my bed and looked at me anxiously.

'Has he gone?'

I couldn't talk, of course. I was done up like a Christmas parcel. So I put my thumb up.

He beamed. 'A knock-out,' he said happily. Then he took hold of my hands, and very gently moved them above my head and put them together.

'What on earth are you doing?' a nurse asked, coming up.

Prince clasped his own hands above his head, and shook them.

'We're the champions!' he said.

Ticket to Heaven

I could not believe I was dead. It was most extraordinary. I had been lying in bed when – pop! I shot up in the air like a champagne cork. Like in the song –

> *'There was an old woman tossed up in a blanket*
> *Seventy times as high as the moon.'*

But I am not an old woman. I am a very rich man, and if the fools I pay to look after me have done this, then they will suffer for it. Just wait till I come down.

But I didn't come down. I remained in the air, bobbing against the ceiling like a helium-filled balloon. Looking down, I could see them bending over my bed. The doctor said, 'He's gone.'

'I'm not gone, you imbecile! I'm up here!' I shouted.

They ignored me. The doctor was filling in a form. The nurse was bending over the – *there was someone in my bed*! In my bed, in my silk pyjamas, with his head on my best, goose-feather pillow. With a great effort, I managed to sink a few inches from the ceiling. Now I could see clearly who was lying on my bed. It was me.

'No!' I shouted. 'It can't be! I'm up here! Don't cover my face, you stupid woman!'

The nurse drew the sheet over my face on the pillow. For a moment, everything went white, as blank as snow; then I could see as clearly as before. They were walking towards the door. I heard my housekeeper say, 'It's a merciful release.' She looked like a cat who is dreaming of the cream pot.

With a sort of furious wiggle, I propelled myself towards her right ear. 'I haven't left you a penny in my will, you ugly old bag!' I shouted.

She gave a little shiver and looked over her shoulder. 'It's cold in here,' she said.

'The chill of death,' said the nurse. 'I don't know about you. I could do with a nice cup of tea.'

'It's *my* tea!' I screamed. 'I forbid you to have any! Do you hear me?'

It was obvious that they did not. They all left the room and I heard them chattering down the stairs. Going to drink my tea, eat my biscuits, the doctor would probably help himself to my whisky! And there was nothing I could do about it. For the first time, alone in my room with my sheeted corpse below me, I realised I was dead.

And I was frightened.

'God forgive me,' I whispered, for I had been a wicked man.

All that night I cowered in the dark room. Waiting for something to happen. Waiting in terror for an avenging angel or grinning devil to fetch me away.

After three months I would have welcomed them. Better hell than this. For three empty months, I drifted around my house, unnoticed, unmourned. Sometimes I wept, though no tears fell. Sometimes I cursed and shouted defiance. No one heard me. You can't imagine what it was like – how cold, how terrible.

People came to the house, the undertakers, the lawyers, my shabby nephew and his thin wife. I fluttered round them, like a moth drawn to bright candles.

'Listen to me! Speak to me! Forgive me!' I wept. 'For pity's sake, speak to me.'

My nephew shivered. His wife turned up her coat collar. The others paid me no attention at all. They ignored me. *Me*! I was – had been – a powerful man. A hard man fighting my way out of the slum where I was born. 'I'm a self-made man,' I had often boasted. But now that manufactured man was dead and buried. I was once again a small child crying for love.

It was odd. I could see and hear. I could move about at will, though I had no feet to run with, nor hands to push myself along. I swam through the air like a tadpole through water. I went through doors like a worm through mud. I could go anywhere I wanted – and there was nowhere I wanted to go.

The house was shut up. Occasionally a house agent brought round prospective buyers. They looked around. They shivered and asked if the house was damp. Nobody heard me. Nobody saw me. I was only a slight chill in the air. No more than that.

'God forgive me, punish me, send me to hell,' I pleaded, 'only don't leave me all alone.'

After a year, I pulled myself together. 'Use your brain, Thomas Warner,' I said (not that I had one, but old habits of speech died hard). 'You are a ghost. Now what do I know about ghosts? Let me see. They haunt the place where they were murdered . . . But I wasn't murdered. I drove my car into a tree when I was drunk, and died in my own bed. What else? They are condemned to stay on earth until they have righted the wrongs they have done –'

If I'd had a heart, it would have sunk to the floor. How could I possibly right all the wrongs I had done? There were hundreds of people I had cheated on my way to the top. I couldn't even remember their names.

I went out into the garden. I could no longer bear the empty house. All night, I wailed with the wind, wept with the rain. It was me you heard beating against your window. It was me you heard moaning at your door. But none of you let me in.

The morning came cold and clear, with a pale sun in the washed sky. I knew now what I must do. I must search the world to find someone I could reach, even if it took a thousand years. I must tell them where my gold lay buried, and beg them to give it to charity. I must buy a ticket to Heaven. There must be someone, somewhere, who could see me.

I found her that afternoon, in a garden not three miles away from my home. She was sitting on a lawn in the sun and reading a book. I looked over the hedge at her without much hope. She was a girl of about fourteen or fifteen, with improbable apricot-coloured hair. Her face was flushed and she sniffed now and then, as if she had a cold or had been crying. She was dressed in the gear they all wear; faded blue denim trousers and a sweatshirt with writing on it – Save the Elephant and the Ant. Ridiculous.

I have always disliked teenagers. There is something about them that makes me want to scratch. They wear silly clothes and giggle. They rush about on noisy motor-bikes, getting in the way of my car. One moment they're drooping around the town with their arms round each other as if in need of support. The next, they're sheer energy, running down the quiet streets of my suburb, leaping up to pluck leaves off the overhanging trees. *My* trees. *My* leaves.

Worst of all, they have no respect for money. Oh, they like spending it, as any parent will tell you, but they're just as likely to give it away to their friends, or to some lost cause – Save the Elephant and the Ant. That's typical. Who cares about the elephant and the ant? They do. That's the trouble with them. They think the world's worth saving.

I would have passed her by, but at that moment she looked up and said, 'Go away!'

'You can see me!' I cried with delight. 'You can see me!'

'Go away!' she said again, and blew her nose on a grubby handkerchief.

I stayed where I was, hovering above the hedge, not wanting to go nearer in case she retreated to the house.

'May I talk to you?' I asked humbly. 'Don't be afraid. I won't hurt you. I just want to ask you something.'

'No.'

'Why not?'

'I'm not allowed to talk to ghosts,' she told me. 'Dad says it's freaky and Ma says it'll put people off me. She means boys, of course. She's wrong, but it's no good telling her. So you'd better go away.'

'Do you always do what your mother says?' I asked, hoping to shame her into rebellion.

She shrugged and muttered, 'It's boring talking to ghosts. They're always moaning about something.'

If I'd had a hand, I'd have slapped her. Sometimes I wonder if I'll ever learn to be good or if I've left it too late.

We sat in silence. At least, she sat on the grass while I floated about five centimetres above the hedge, looking down at her. There was a small hole in her sweatshirt and her denim trousers were frayed; her hair was like a flaming bush. She didn't look like a girl who bothered about her appearance, but you couldn't always tell. Sometimes it amuses them to go around in rags.

Then I noticed the silver bracelets on her left arm. There must have been over a dozen of them, thin and cheap enough, some of them bent out of shape.

'If you do me a small favour,' I said, 'you can have a gold bracelet.'

'Don't like gold,' she said.

Didn't like gold! What can you do with a person like that? I suppose the colour doesn't match her eyes.

I kept my temper. 'You can buy things with gold,' I pointed out patiently, 'whatever you like. Or you could give it to charity, if that's what you go for. You might even be able to save the green-spotted bog beetle.'

She laughed at that. She looked very pretty when she laughed.

'You made that up,' she said, 'there's no such creature.'

She wasn't stupid. I was glad she had a sense of humour. I almost liked her. It was an odd feeling, a sort of warmth I'd never felt before, not even when I was as young as she was.

'Is there anything you want?' I asked gently.

The laughter left her face.

'I want Billy,' she said. 'I want Billikins back.'

Who could be worth more than gold to her?

'Your boyfriend? Your brother?' I asked.

'He's my cat,' she cried, and burst into tears.

A cat. Only a cat. I should have guessed it would be something like that, seeing the sort of girl she was. A black cat, she told me, with one white paw and a white tip to its tail. He'd been missing for a week.

'If I find him, will you promise –'

'Yes, yes!' she broke in eagerly, without waiting to find

out what. She would have promised almost anything, and all for a cat. I'd never cared for cats. I'd never felt like this about any living creature. Had I missed something? Too late now.

I told her what I wanted her to do. 'When I was alive,' I said, 'I had converted a large part of my money into gold and diamonds, and hidden it in the grounds of my house –'

'To avoid death duty, I suppose,' she said, with a hint of disapproval that infuriated me.

'No. There is nobody I want to leave anything to,' I said, and she had the impertinence to look sorry for me. 'I wanted to avoid tax, and have something I could see easily anywhere in the world. Never mind that! It's nothing to do with you. Listen to me. I'll tell you how to find it. You can keep ten per cent, but you must promise to give the rest to charity, do you understand?'

She understood all right. 'Trying to buy your way into Heaven?' she asked. 'It won't work.'

'How do you know? It might.'

She shook her head and quoted that piece about the rich man and the eye of the needle. I hoped she was wrong.

'It's worth trying,' I said.

'It'd be stealing,' she said doubtfully. 'It must belong to someone.'

'The taxman,' I said. 'Do you prefer the taxman to your cat?'

'No.'

'So you'll do it?'

I was glad to see she had the sense to say, '*After* you've got me Billikins back.'

Oh, that suburb full of cats; tabby cats, ginger cats, black cats and tortoiseshell. Lying in the sun, stalking in the long grass, climbing up trees, stealing from dustbins. But no Billikins.

I called his name and the cats heard me. Whiskered heads turned, yellow eyes glared. They saw me and they spat.

'Billikins! Billikins!' I shouted, and the cats watched me and growled in their throats.

I nearly missed him. I was drifting over the garden of a large, old house, peering down through the weeds and the brambles, when I heard a faint mewing.

'Billikins?'

'Miaow!'

Where was he? I sank towards the ground. Brambles dragged through me with an odd, tickling sensation. Then I saw the well. The cover was lying on the ground beside it, the wood half rotted away. I peered into the dark hole and saw, far below, two orange eyes like drowned suns staring up at me.

Billikins. How was I to get him out? I had no hands. I couldn't even lift a feather. I must go back to the girl and tell her where her cat was. I was about to leave the garden when I heard a voice say, 'What can I do for you, my friend?'

I turned and saw a grey-haired man in a neat grey suit.

'You can see me?' I cried.

'I can indeed,' he said, smiling. 'I'm a sensitive. Nicholas Fry, at your service. Always glad to help the dear departed. Why have you come to me? Is it a message for a loved one?'

I looked at him. I doubt if I would have trusted him when I was alive, but then I had trusted no one. And it was either him or the teenage girl. My instincts were against the girl. She was young, with a head stuffed full of dreams and ideals, and all her mistakes still to be made.

On the other hand, the man looked sharp enough, in spite of the nonsense about the 'dear departed'. He'd be willing to help me for a fee, with none of the trouble of rescuing a cat. I didn't need the girl now.

'I have a proposition to put to you,' I said.

I told him about my buried gold. I offered him a quarter share to keep for himself. I saw his eyes widen.

'Very generous,' he said.

'I want the rest to go to charity.'

'Charity, eh? Very nice. That's what I like, someone with a kind heart,' he said, rubbing his hands together. 'Any particular charity in mind?'

I thought of the girl and said, 'A charity that rescues endangered species.'

He nodded his head. 'I see, sir. Very nice. Save the whale, that sort of thing – elephants, sir? Right you are. I'll do that for you. Where is this gold of yours, then?'

'Just a minute – ' I said.

I don't know why I didn't tell him and have done with it. I had to trust someone. Why did I keep thinking of the girl? I saw her laughing over the green-spotted bog beetle. I remembered how she'd looked sorry for me. She had wanted to help me, I knew that. It was not only her cat. She had wanted to save the elephant and the ant *and* the ghost, too.

'There's a cat down your well,' I said.

He wasn't interested. 'Wretched creatures. Always getting in where they shouldn't. It can stay there. The well's dry. It won't come to any harm.'

'It will starve. I want you to bring it out.'

He gave in immediately, smiling and saying, 'Now that's kind. An animal lover, are we, sir? That's what I like to see.'

Then he fetched a basket and a rope from the house, and we let it down the well. The little cat cowered away from the basket and spat. The man said something under his breath.

'I'll entice him into the basket,' I said. 'Wait here.'

The bottom of the well was choked with dead leaves and rubbish. Water gleamed through the lattice-work of twigs on which the cat crouched. He was shivering and his eyes watched me as I floated down. He liked me even less than he liked the basket. He spat and his claws raked through me.

I laughed. So small and full of courage. His fur was spiky, his legs thin as needles and his sides concave, but what brave defiance blazed in his eyes.

I darted towards him as he lashed out again. His paw went right through me and he fell on his nose. Round and round we went as I tried to chase him into the basket.

'Hurry up!' the old man called.

I was – or had been – an obstinate man. I was not going to give up. I liked the brave little cat. I hovered above his head. He leaped up, trying to catch me, and missed. Now I danced round him like a demented fly and he sprang after me, scrabbling at the wall, bouncing off the twigs, leaping over the basket. His eyes were gleaming and I heard a loud rattle coming from his throat. He was purring. It was a game now. I had found a playmate at last.

'You're wasting time!' the man shouted.

I whizzed past the cat's nose and darted into the basket. He sprang in after me, and the old man began to pull us up. I could feel the little cat's heart beating with terror as the basket swayed and bumped against the walls.

'It's all right,' I whispered. 'You're safe.'

He looked at me with huge yellow eyes. Perhaps he understood, for he did not move. Now we were out in the air. The old man grabbed Billikins roughly by the scruff of his neck and dumped him on the ground. He streaked away without a backwards glance. I hoped he knew his way home.

'Now what about our agreement?' the old man asked.

I told him where I had hidden my gold. In which garden, beneath which tree, how far down. As I spoke I saw an expression I knew only too well come into his face, an expression I had seen in my own mirror. Greed.

'You can keep half!' I cried wildly. 'The rest is for charity, remember?'

He smiled and rubbed his hands together. I had thought I could trust him. How could I have been so horribly mistaken? His little eyes glinted redly, as if lit by sparks of fire. His smile vanished into folds of fat. He began to laugh until the earth shook. I backed away from him. He was evil, a devil. I had gambled and I had lost. I'd have done far better to have trusted a child.

I let the wind blow me where it would. Down little

streets I whirled, with the dead leaves and the rubbish. Litter, that's all I was, discarded, unwanted. I must have gone round in circles, because at last I came to a hedge I recognised. It was night now. Her forgotten book lay on the moonlit lawn. I wondered if Billikins had got home safely.

Then I saw him, stepping daintily over the grass towards me. His eyes were brighter than sovereigns. His whiskers smelled of cream.

'Hullo, Billikins,' I said.

He blinked at me in greeting, and twitched his tail like a finger beckoning. Then he ran off.

I followed him. He seemed to know where he was going, running swiftly and silently, his black fur silvered by the moonlight. He led me to an open square, then stopped, sat down and began to wash his paws.

'Funny sort of angel you've got,' said a voice.

I was no longer alone. Suddenly the night was crowded with beings like myself. Ghosts, I suppose you would call them. To me they were what I'd wanted and never had. Friends.

'Glad you got here in the end.'

'Thought you'd never make it.'

'We've been waiting ages.'

I looked up gratefully at the sky. The night was bright with stars.

The Paper-boy

Robert glanced at his reflection in every shop window he passed. How different he looked. His clothes were all new. His shoes were shining. Last month he had worn frayed denims, a sweatshirt and grubby sneakers, but last month he had been a schoolboy. Now he was a worker with a job to go to.

'Some job!' Pete Wrightson, his school enemy, had sneered last term. 'Helping out in your rich uncle's shop. Yes, sir, no, sir, three bags full, sir! Sweeping the floor, making the tea! Perhaps if you're very good, he'll allow you to polish his precious furniture.'

'Everyone has to start at the bottom,' Robert had said, quoting his uncle. Even to himself, he sounded prim. Pete laughed.

'Is that what he told you? Ha! That figures. Cheap labour, that's all you are to him. I bet he's paying you peanuts.'

'It's more than you get as a paper-boy!' Robert retorted.

'How long does it take to deliver papers? Next to no time if you're quick like me. But you'll be working full-time for your peanuts. Proper little wage slave, you'll be. And everything you do wrong, your uncle will tell your mum. That wouldn't suit me.'

'Don't take any notice,' Robert's friends told him, 'he's just jealous because he hasn't got a rich uncle to give him a job. Didn't you see how sour he looked when you told us?'

'There are times I'd like to hit him,' Robert confessed. 'He's always tried to spoil things for me. I don't know why.'

'He just doesn't like you.'

'But what have I done?'

'Nothing. It happens that way sometimes,' they said. 'Never mind. We like you. And you won't ever have to see him again once you've left school.'

'No, I won't,' Robert agreed, thankfully.

It was not vanity that made Robert keep glancing at his reflection in the windows as he passed. It was the need for reassurance. His uncle's shop was very grand, more of a furniture store than a mere shop. It had thick blue carpet everywhere, fresh flowers on the desks, and gold letters above the glass doors, saying, 'Harold Penn. Fine furniture. Carpets. China.' The other assistants (all except for Miss Bell, who was plump and pink) were much older than Robert, and as sharp as pins.

All last week, his mother had nagged him, making him nervous. 'I want you to get into the habit of thinking of your appearance, Robert,' she'd said, when he'd complained that he was not even due to go to work until Monday. 'Now, have you scrubbed your fingernails today?'

'Yes, Mum.'

'And combed your hair?'

'Yes.'

'And brushed your shoes?'

'*Yes*!'

'Remind me to buy you a little mirror to keep in your breast pocket –'

'Oh, *Mum*!'

'You must be neat, dear,' she told him. 'And polite. Remember, you'll be on show. Whatever you do, don't cheek your uncle. He's the only rich uncle you've got.'

'I won't cheek him, Mum. I wouldn't dare,' Robert had said ruefully.

He was glad when Monday came at last. It was a bright, windy day – 'Don't forget to smooth your hair down before you go in!' his mother had shouted after him as he hurried off.

He sighed. Perhaps Pete was right and it was better to be a paper-boy, cycling carelessly through the sunny morning streets. Immediately, as if the thought of a paper-boy had conjured one up like a devil from hell, there was a soft swish of wheels on the pavement, and there was Pete, cycling past him, tapping Robert's head with a rolled up newspaper as he went and shrieking with laughter.

'Look at Lord Muck! Ain't you grand? Off to scrub floors in your Sunday best? Don't get yourself dirty now. Your hair's in a bit of a mess.' He had circled round and was coming back towards Robert, still holding the rolled up newspaper in his hand, 'Here! Let me comb it for you!' He whisked Robert's hair with the paper, as if beating an egg. 'That's better!'

Not wanting to provoke a fight, not in his new clothes, Robert merely laughed. 'Thanks,' he called and hoped Pete would leave it at that.

And Pete would have done, had not a man coming along the pavement towards them waved his walking stick at him, and shouted, 'Get off the pavement! Yes, I'm talking to you! You with the spots and the bicycle!'

Pete was sensitive about his acne. He flushed crimson.

He wanted to hit the man, but the man was too big. It was easier to wait until he had gone, and hit Robert instead.

So it was that Robert arrived at work on his first day with his new clothes dusty and creased, two buttons off his shirt and his tie missing completely.

'What happened, Robert?' his uncle asked quietly, seeing the boy's pale face smudged with bruises and dirt.

Robert told him.

'Pete? Is that the Lynton boy? Which newsagent does he work for?' his uncle asked.

'I don't know,' Robert lied, already regretting having given Pete's name. 'It doesn't matter. He won't do it again. Honestly, please don't –'

'Leave it to me,' his uncle said.

'But I can manage –'

'That's enough. I've told you, I'll handle it. Now tidy yourself up as best you can, and then go and help Mr Brant in the storeroom where you won't be seen. We can't have our customers thinking we beat up our new assistants, can we?'

There was nothing Robert could do but smile and mumble inaudibly.

Oh well, he thought, as he washed his face and combed his hair, it's not my fault. I didn't start the fight. Pete did. If he gets into trouble, it's his own fault.

* * *

The next morning Robert looked round every corner for Pete, but there was no sign of his enemy on his yellow bicycle. It doesn't mean anything, he told himself. He might have overslept. He might be going a different way. It doesn't mean he's lost his job.

Two days later, however, there was a new paper-boy, with a loud whistle, curly black hair and the same yellow bicycle.

'Hey, what's happened to Pete?' Robert called.

'He's gone!' the boy shouted back. 'I've got his job now.'

'Why did he leave?'

'Dunno,' the boy said and cycled away, leaving Robert feeling miserable and guilty.

Surely nobody would sack a boy because of one complaint? Or would they? Uncle Harold could be very persuasive. Pete's family were poor. Everyone at school had said so. Pete couldn't afford to lose his job. Poor Pete, he'd be wild –

He'll be wild with me! Robert realised.

He began to feel more sorry for himself than for Pete. Pete would want revenge. He'd beat him up. He'd make him lose his job, just when he was beginning to enjoy it. How Pete could achieve this, Robert didn't know, but he was sure Pete would find a way somehow.

I'll have to be careful, he thought.

It was a bright, blowy day. A sheet of ragged newspaper suddenly lifted into the air before him, making him jump. It went jiggling down the pavement. The wind played with it, turning it this way and that. Two long tatters leaped up like kicking legs, and it assumed the shape of a dancing boy, a jeering, sneering newspaper-boy.

Suddenly it caught against a lamppost. Robert hurried forward, meaning to snatch it up and push it into the litter bin. But he was too late. A freakish gust of wind peeled it off the lamppost and flung it straight at him.

The newspaper hung briefly before his eyes, showing a photograph of a young man's face staring out at him, the eyes wide and terrified, the mouth open as if screaming. The paper twisted again and now he saw part of a headline in big black print – DEATH. Before he could read any more, it was gone, blowing up into the sky, twisting and twirling until it came to rest high above his head, caught in the branches of a tree.

He was late for work that morning, having spent too long throwing stones into the tree in an unsuccessful attempt to dislodge the piece of newspaper. When he arrived, breathless and rumpled, his uncle reproached him.

'I hope this isn't going to become a habit, Robert,' he said.

'I'm sorry, Uncle Harold. I was held up.'

'You should make allowances for possible delays. Better to plan to arrive half an hour early than be five minutes late. And by the way, I thought I told you not to call me uncle while we are at work. Call me Mr Penn.'

'Yes, Mr Penn. I'm sorry, Mr Penn. It won't happen again, Mr Penn,' Robert promised, conscious that two of the other assistants were smirking in the background.

'Don't overdo it, you foolish boy,' his uncle said. 'Well, get to work now. We've wasted enough time.'

Flustered, Robert could not remember what he was supposed to be doing that day and started hurrying off in the wrong direction, only to be called back.

'Where do you think you're going? Wake up, boy! You're supposed to be helping Miss Bell with the new delivery of china today. Remember?'

'Oh yes. Sorry.'

'Hurry along then.'

Robert was glad he was with Miss Bell that morning. Miss Bell was soft and young and sympathetic.

'Don't take any notice of your uncle, love. He doesn't mean any harm. He's often a bit tetchy in the mornings. Indigestion, I expect. Too much guzzling fatty bacon and fried bread. Now, you unload this crate while I tick the items off on my list – careful! You nearly had that jug over.' She looked at him curiously. 'Why, your hands are all shaky. Look, I'd better unload while you tick. It won't matter if you drop the pencil. Cheer up. Don't let your uncle get you down. You're as white as a sheet. You're not ill, are you?'

'No! No, I'm all right. Honestly. It was just – I had a bit of a fright on the way here.'

'A fright? What sort of fright?'

What could he say? I was frightened by a piece of newspaper? There was a photograph on it of a screaming face. I knew the face! I recognised it. It was mine. And there was a big headline saying DEATH . . .

No, He couldn't tell her. She'd think he was mad.

'I was nearly run over,' he invented. 'By a bicycle. It came up behind me on the pavement.'

'They shouldn't ride on the pavements,' she said, shaking her head. 'Not that you can blame them, what with the traffic on the roads. Still, it gives you a nasty turn, doesn't it, when they whizz by like ghosts on wheels.'

'Ghosts!'

'So quiet, I mean. You can hardly hear them and then they're gone,' she said. Her eyes, though kind, were still curious. To distract her, he asked, 'Have you got a newspaper?'

'In my bag in the cloakroom,' she told him. 'You'll have to wait for our lunch-break, I'm afraid. I'll let you have it then.'

There was nothing in her paper. No photograph of a young man screaming. No headline like the one he'd seen.

'Have you found what you're looking for?' Miss Bell asked.

'No. It must be the wrong paper.'

'What was it you wanted?'

'I didn't want it!' he said sharply, and she looked at him in surprise. 'Sorry. It was a headline saying DEATH, in big black letters. I wanted to read . . . I wanted to find out who . . . But I couldn't see any more. Just DEATH.'

'Plenty of death in all the newspapers,' Miss Bell told him, 'death and murder and violence. You mustn't let it get you down, love. No good getting yourself depressed. Turn to the sports pages, that's what my boyfriend does. Mind you, he's glum enough when Arsenal lose. You can't count on anything. Here, have a chocolate biscuit.'

She began bringing him something every day, a chocolate biscuit, or an apple, or five strawberries wrapped up in a big leaf. She was worried about him.

'You're fading away, love,' she told him. 'I don't like the look of you at all. I think you should see your doctor.'

'That's what Mum says. She worries too. But there's nothing wrong with me.'

'Then why are you so thin and white? You look haunted.'

'I'm not!' he cried, too quickly, too loudly.

He tried to smile at her but his face felt as stiff as a skull's. He could tell that he had not convinced her. How did she guess, he wondered. You look haunted, she'd said. Did it show so plainly?

He wished he could confide in her, but he couldn't tell anybody. It sounded too stupid, to be haunted every day by a ghost made out of torn newspaper. Whichever new way he went to work, it made no difference. Always, a sudden wind would blow, and there it would be, twisting and turning, showing him first a photograph of his own face, screaming in terror; and next the big black letters saying DEATH. Is that what Miss Bell had seen, the word DEATH shadowing him?

He could not face the streets again, and decided to go through Highgate Wood, even though it would take him longer to reach his uncle's shop. Once well away from the road, the suburban woods were peaceful. He left the path and walked between the trees. How quiet it was. Sparse green grass, bleached flowers and small yellow toadstools replaced the torn paper and cigarette stubs. There were no people in sight, only birds. Crows turned their heads to look at him, and strutted calmly away. A magpie flew by.

'One for sorrow,' his mother always said.

He looked around, hoping to see a second magpie to

break the ill luck. Something moved in a nearby bush. He turned and saw it was not a bird on a low branch: it was the crumpled newspaper. Somebody had torn it roughly into the shape of a boy and spread it out on the bush for him to see. Pete! It must have been Pete! Who else would have done it?

He stared at the figure. Wind crept through the leaves and fluttered its arms and legs. Small print greyed its face; it had no eyes. Where they should have been, black letters said, most horribly, HATE! On its body, he saw again the photograph of the screaming youth. Terror distorted its features, but he knew whose face it was. It was his own. REVENGE! the headline shouted.

The wind blew stronger, and the figure lurched sideways. A paper hand reached out and touched his cheek, as if claiming him.

Robert screamed. He ran through the trees, down the path and out of the woods, screaming all the way. A large brown dog sprang out of the bushes and ran barking at his heels. A red-faced woman ran after him, shouting, 'He won't hurt you! He's a good boy!'

It was difficult to tell whether she meant Pete or the dog.

Robert ran on blindly. He was going so fast that he exploded out of the woods, across the pavement and into the road before he could stop himself.

All around him, he heard traffic roar and shriek. The ground trembled beneath his feet. Then he saw Pete in front of him, standing in the path of an advancing lorry, his eyes bewildered with terror, his face as pale as death. Without thinking, Robert flung himself forward and tried to push the other boy towards the safety of the opposite curb. His hands touched nothing and he fell. Something hard hit him on the side of his head, and the world vanished.

When he first opened his eyes, he thought he was dead, lying in a narrow grave so full of green leaves and pale flowers that he could hardly see the brown earth they grew from. He blinked and his eyes cleared. Now he saw he was lying in a hospital bed, surrounded on three sides by floral curtains. There was a chair by his bed but nobody sat on it. Beyond the curtains, he heard footsteps passing and voices in the distance, but nobody came.

His head ached. He felt a bandage round it and some sort of medical smell clung to his fingers like a perfume.

What had happened?

He remembered walking through the woods, the small flowers, the pale toadstools, the green leaves and . . . the paper-boy! He sat up quickly and the movement sent his memories whirling round and round like fragments in a kaleidoscope; green leaves, a single magpie for sorrow, the word DEATH, a hand touching his cheek. Now something huge and dark came roaring towards him and his enemy and he pushed, he pushed the empty air –

Robert lay back, shivering. What had he done? He couldn't remember. The kaleidoscope went round again; the magpie, the dog, the leaves, and the word DEATH. Had he killed Pete? No! He didn't want Pete to be dead. He turned his face into his pillows and began to cry for his enemy as if for the loss of an old friend.

'Is it hurting?' a voice asked. 'Do you want me to call a nurse? Or your mum? She's down in the canteen, stuffing her face. She got tired of waiting for you to wake up.'

It was Pete's voice. Robert held his breath, afraid to look round for fear of what he should see.

'I thought I'd better stay around in case you woke up and felt lonely all by yourself,' the voice went on, 'wasn't that nice of me? I got to be nice to you now. Going to be a bit of a drag, that. I'm not used to being nice to people. Oh well.'

Robert turned his head slowly. It was Pete all right. Pete with his spotty face and his sharp greenish eyes. Not a boy made out of newspaper. Not a ghost. And yet – how bloodless he looked. His face gleamed against the shadowy curtains, as pale as fungus on a dark tree.

'You tried to save my life,' Pete went on. 'Much too late, mind you, but you tried. You could've been killed.

Funny, I'd always thought you disliked me. What made you do it, chum?'

'I don't know. I just did. I never really hated you, not *hated*! But you were always teasing me . . . I didn't mean you to lose your job, Pete. I tried to stop my uncle, but he wouldn't listen. And I certainly didn't want you dead.'

Pete laughed, his eyes glinting like broken glass, sharp and cold. 'Bad luck,' he said, 'because that's what you've got. Me dead.'

'I don't understand!'

'You always were a blockhead! Fancy risking your life trying to save a ghost. I died three weeks ago, mate. Been haunting you ever since, didn't you even notice? Talk about thick! I should've haunted the lorry driver. I bet he would've noticed me. But I thought it would be more fun teasing you.'

He stood up and smiled down at Robert, quite kindly. 'Don't worry. I won't tease you no more. Pity. I always enjoyed it. You know, if I hadn't got myself run over, we could've been friends. It wasn't your uncle lost me my job, it was a lorry in King's Road. Squashed me flat three weeks ago. Here, read all about it!'

He tossed a newspaper on to the bed and then he was gone, and there were only the flowered curtains stirring slightly as if in a cold draught.

It was the local paper, an old one with last month's

date on it. Three weeks old, in fact. Robert picked it up. It was opened at one of the middle pages. Robert saw the blurred photograph of a young man's face staring out at him. the man had his mouth open as if he was screaming. It was not his face. It was not Pete's face. It was the photograph of the leading actor in a play called DEATH COMES TO VISIT. It was only later that he noticed a small headline tucked away in a corner at the bottom of the page, saying, *Paper-boy Killed in Road Accident.*

Tears came to his eyes. 'We could've been friends,' Pete had said, but it was too late now. Could you be friends with a ghost?

Orpheus and the Underworld

Long ago and far away, there was a boy called Orpheus. His father was Apollo, the sun god, and out from morning till night; while his mother was an important lady, with little time to spare.

'Run along and play, Orpheus,' she always said, 'can't you see I'm busy?'

One night, when Apollo came home, he brought his son a present.

'Run along and play, Orpheus,' he said, smiling.

Orpheus looked at his present. It was an odd-shaped

wooden box, with a long handle and four strings over a hole in the middle. Perhaps there was something inside?

Orpheus pulled at the strings. To his surprise they made a sweet sound, each one different – plonk, plunk, plenk, plink.

'Really, Apollo,' his mother said, 'my poor head! Did you have to give him a lute?'

But Orpheus would not be parted from his new toy. He took it to his room and played with it every day.

Soon the sounds he made were so beautiful that his mother took her fingers out of her ears and stopped to listen.

His father, going about his daily work, heard the music echoing through the sky and stopped to listen. The sun rolled out from behind a cloud like a great golden wheel and stopped to listen.

'For goodness' sake, Orpheus,' his mother cried, 'play another tune, or your father won't get home tonight.'

'For the earth's sake, Orpheus,' the farmers cried, 'play another tune and send the sun about its business. Our corn is sizzling in our fields. Our streams run dry. Our silly cows won't come home to be milked.'

So Orpheus played a night tune, and the sun went down with a sigh. The moon and stars came out to listen, and his father came home to bed.

'You know, Apollo,' his mother said, as they lay listening in the spangled dark, 'our boy is really very good.

He's got talent. See how the stars dance to his music. I've never seen anything like it. Even the moon is nodding and beaming. I wouldn't be at all surprised if he isn't famous one day. What a good idea of mine it was to give him a lute.'

Apollo smiled at this, but said nothing.

One spring, Orpheus went out into the fields and began to play love songs. The trees shivered with delight and shuffled nearer to listen, sighing with their leaves. Birds spread their wings against the wind and hung motionless above his head. The shy deer crowded round him, and the fish stood on their tails in the hushed river, listening with open mouths.

His music was so full of longing that it moved even the hearts of stones, and they rolled down from the mountains to gather round his feet.

'That's all very well,' his mother said, 'but he's wasting his time in the fields. Why can't he give a proper concert in the palace,' she added. 'With tickets.'

'That's all very well, Orpheus,' the farmers cried, 'but your animals trample our crops. Your stones have broken our fences. Your trees stand in the way of our ploughs. Play another tune, and let us get on with our work.'

But Orpheus would not listen to them. He went on playing love songs with a silly smile on his face.

'For goodness' sake,' his mother sighed, 'I wish he'd marry a nice sensible girl and settle down.'

But the girl Orpheus loved and married was sweet and silly, and always laughing. Her name was Eurydice and she was beautiful. Her skin was the colour of mountain honey and her hair was as black as midnight. She loved to wander barefoot through the meadows, picking wild flowers to bring home to him.

'This really won't do, Orpheus,' his mother said, 'your wife has a position to keep up. She should go out into the world and make a great career for herself. Like me. Or she should stay at home and look after her household. Your servants are getting lazy. There's dust on that table. I can see it from here! All this wandering about like a gipsy, smiling at everyone she meets, it's not safe. There are wolves in the woods, just waiting to snap up a silly girl. She'll get into trouble one of these days, you tell her from me.'

But Eurydice only laughed when Orpheus told her.

'Your mother's too fond of being dramatic,' she said, tossing her long black hair, 'the wild creatures love me. No one would dream of doing me harm.'

But one day, when Eurydice was out walking, a rude shepherd jumped out at her from behind a bush, shouting, and tried to grab hold of her.

Eurydice was frightened.

She ran away. She ran through the meadows, calling for Orpheus. She ran so quickly that she trod on a sleeping snake before it had time to wake up and slide out of the way.

The snake rose up in fury, coil after coil after coil unwinding, into a long, sinuous, shimmering string of anger.

It bit her and she died.

Poor Orpheus. His beautiful Eurydice lies cold in a bed of long grass. Her face is as white as bone now and her hair as black as mourning.

Then Pluto, the grim god of the Underworld comes to claim her, as is his right now that she is dead. He carries her down, down, down to his dark kingdom under the earth.

Orpheus looked for her everywhere. In the fields. In the woods. On the cold tops of mountains. But he could not find her.

'Eurydice is dead, Orpheus,' his father told him gently. 'It's no good looking for her any longer. She is a grey ghost in the Underworld now. Pluto holds her prisoner, as is his right.'

Orpheus went home. The wild flowers had faded in their vases. There was no sound of laughter in the empty rooms.

He sat down and cried, and played sad songs. Hearing

him, the sky could not stop weeping in sympathy, and the rivers overflowed their banks.

'Play another tune, Orpheus,' the farmers begged, 'our fields are flooded. Our cows stand knee-deep in water. Our ploughs rust.'

But Orpheus would not listen to them.

He played such loud, wild songs of grief that a grey ghost in the Underworld pushed back a trapdoor in order to listen to them.

What was that? A thin sound, like a silver needle, pricked through the clamorous music.

Orpheus stopped playing. There it came again. A faint, sweet voice calling, 'Orpheus! Orpheus! Orpheus!'

Orpheus jumped to his feet. He stared down at the dark hole. He could see nothing.

'Eurydice!' he called.

'Orpheus!' the voice answered.

How cold it sounded. How far away. Was it really Eurydice?

He crouched down by the hole, and stared. Now he could see a ladder, leading down and down.

'I must go and find her,' he said, but his voice shook with fear.

When he was a child, his father had told him about the Underworld. Told him that only the dead were allowed to enter that dark kingdom, and it was well guarded.

'How?' he had asked.

'By hideous monsters, Orpheus,' his father had said, 'by creatures so foul and filthy that my lips shrivel to speak of them . . .'

'Oh dear,' Orpheus said, remembering. He took a step back.

A reproachful sigh rose from the trapdoor. 'Orpheus! Oh, Orpheus!'

'Coming! he shouted, and quickly, before his courage could fail him again, he stepped down into the dark.

Down he went,

and down,

and down.

Suddenly little flames sprang out all around him, as if a thousand invisible hands were holding up candles to light his way.

Clutching his lute to his chest to protect it, he hurried on –

down,

and down,

and down,

and down,

and down,

and down.

Now the flames went out, as if ashamed to show the littered dust beneath the green crust of the earth. Orpheus went on –

down

and down,

and down

until at last he found himself on a small wooden jetty. In front of him there was only water, silent and still, stretching out into the darkness.

The river Styx, he remembered. His father had told him there was a ferryman – Charon! That was his name.

'Ahoy there!' Orpheus called. 'Charon, ahoy!'

The echoes died away. The black water began to ripple. Little waves splashed against the jetty.

A boat appeared out of the misty dark. A man was standing in it. He looked hard at Orpheus, and held the boat away from the jetty with his oar.

'Who are you? Why do you call me?'

'I'm Orpheus, and I want to go to the Underworld.'

'Are you dead?' the man asked. 'Only the dead are allowed to cross here.'

'I might just as well be dead,' Orpheus said sadly, 'without my Eurydice.'

'Hmm,' the man said, unimpressed, 'open your mouth.'

Surprised, Orpheus did as he was told.

'Empty,' the man said in disgust, 'the dead always have a gold coin put in their mouths to pay for their passage. Didn't you even know that? You're an imposter. Go away.'

Orpheus began to play on his lute. He played a sailor's song. He sang of a great ship flying before a storm, her sails cracking in the wind. Huge waves bared their white teeth and snapped at her heels. Faster and faster she sails. Suddenly the look-out screams down from the crow's nest –

'Well, go on,' the ferryman said, as Orpheus stopped, 'what happened? Was she wrecked?'

'Take me across,' Orpheus said, 'and I'll finish my song.'

So the ferryman took Orpheus across the river Styx,

and Orpheus played home-coming music; the gentle rocking of a tired ship safe in harbour, the welcoming crackle of a log fire in a warm inn, the sound of hot rum being poured into a tankard, held in a cold sailor's hand.

'Ah, that was a good song, Orpheus,' the ferryman said, 'play it again.'

But Orpheus jumped ashore, and went on with his journey.

He turned a corner. In front of him, completely blocking his way, was a stinking, dribbling monster. An enormous dog with three heads, each uglier than its neighbour. Three pairs of whirling, burning eyes. Three gaping jaws with too many teeth to count. Three great tongues ready to lick the blood from his bones.

'Good dog,' Orpheus said nervously, and jumped back as it snapped at him, growling most horribly.

Standing well out of reach, Orpheus began to play on his lute. He played a song of a cat, high up in a tree, spitting down insults.

So vivid was his song that the great dog began to leap into the air, its three jaws snapping and grinding. Higher and higher went the cat music, and higher and higher the creature leaped. At last, exhausted, it collapsed on the ground, its three tongues hanging out like wet rags.

Now Orpheus played a dreamy tune, of a tired dog lying in front of the fire after a hard day's hunting.

The six red eyes shut sleepily, and did not see Orpheus as he walked past.

'Phew!' Orpheus said. 'I hope I see nothing worse –'

He broke off, staring.

In front of him, grinning angrily, were three terrible women. Their teeth were as sharp and as pointed as pins. Their grey hair stood up on end, and their eyes glared at him with such fury that he could not believe that they wished him well.

'What have we got here?' one of them croaked, licking her lips.

Quickly, Orpheus began to play.

He played a dance tune, a fast tune, a whirling, twirling, jigging, hopping-up-and-down tune.

The three ghastly ladies could not stop their feet from following his music. The began to caper and prance and skip.

'And a one and a two and a swing your partner round . . .'

Round and round they went, faster and faster, until their faces were as purple as plums, and sweat blinded their eyes.

'Cree-um-plonk!'

Orpheus ended with a discord, and the women fell down in a tangle, their skimpy arms and legs woven tightly together like twigs in a nest.

'Get yourselves out of that,' Orpheus said, and he

walked away, feeling pleased with himself. Really, he was doing rather well . . .

Iron claws gripped his back and lifted him into the air.

Looking up in terror, he saw he was held by an extraordinary creature, with the body of a bird and the head of a foul woman.

Hanging upside down, he could not play his lute. Desperately, he sang,

'Now leaves have come a-leaping
From bud and branch and seedling,
And buttercups are gold,
It's time to think of nesting,
Of sitting down and resting,
Don't let your eggs get cold.'

She looked round, as if half-seeing leaves sprouting from the dark rocks. Her face became broody. But she did not let him go.

'Take care, the sun is sinking,
The one-eyed daisy's blinking,
The wings of night unfold.
It's time to spread your cover,
O, feather-beddy mother,
Don't let your eggs get cold.'

* * *

Letting him go, she fluttered down to the floor of the cave. There she sat, eyes closed, ruffling her feathers protectively over three round lumps of coal. Orpheus walked on.

Now he found himself in a vast cave. There, in the middle, standing on a rock, was a metallic figure, whose face was as hard as an iron hammer, and whose eyes blazed with cold fires.

Orpheus was too wise to mistake him for another monster. He bowed politely to Pluto, the dread god of the Underworld, recognising him from his father's description. ('He looks rather like our kitchen stove,' his father had said.)

'How dare you come here, Orpheus,' Pluto cried, his voice roaring in his throat like fire in a chimney and smoke coming out of his ears.

'Please, mighty king,' Orpheus begged, going down on his knees. 'Great Pluto, you have so many subjects. Surely you won't miss just one? Let me take Eurydice back with me, and I swear we'll return to you in the end, as all must do.'

Then he played a tune of such beauty and tenderness, that the god's iron face cracked and tears hissed in his burning eyes.

'Oh, very well, take her,' he muttered. Then, repenting of his softness, he added, 'Only don't look at her until you are both out of my kingdom. Or I will take her back. Go on, quick, before I change my mind.'

Orpheus led Eurydice along the endless passages, round corners and through tunnels, past the still sleeping monsters and the tangled Furies; guiding her through the darkness by the sound of his lute.

Now and then, he stilled the strings with his hand, and listened. There was thick ash underfoot and he could hear no sound of footsteps.

'Are you still there, Eurydice?' he called.

'Here I am,' she answered.

On and on they walked through the thick shadows, with the soft, muffling ash underfoot and only the ribbon of his music floating behind him to guide his love.

'Are you still there? Eurydice?' he called.

'Here I am,' she answered.

At last he saw a grey light in front of them. It grew brighter and brighter, until suddenly a great arch appeared in the rocks ahead. He could see sunlight and green grass and a silly sheep looking up in surprise.

'We've done it, Eurydice!' he cried, turning round to smile at her.

Too soon.

With a cry of despair, she was torn from him.

*

Orpheus tried to get back into the Underworld, but all ways were shut to him now. The ferryman refused to take him. Orpheus begged and wept and fell on his knees, but Charon shook his head.

'It's more than my job's worth,' he said, 'Pluto has forbidden it. You had your chance and you mucked it. Go away, Orpheus.'

Now Orpheus sits on the banks of a river, and fills it with his tears. He will not listen when people try to comfort him. He pushes his mother away. He turns his back on his father. He will not speak to anybody.

All he does is fill the air with his complaints until the sky rings with them.

At first, the fierce tigers weep to hear him. The cruel thorns melt and drip from their stems like tears. The hard stones of the river bank become as soft as porridge. And Orpheus goes on crying.

Then the tigers yawn and shrug, and go about their business. The thorns harden again and prick him. The stones bruise his feet when he moves.

And still Orpheus goes on crying.

One day, some Thracian maidens came to comfort him. They were young and pretty, and had a good opinion of themselves.

'Cheer up, Orpheus,' one of them said, 'forget your

Eurydice. There are more beautiful fish in the river than ever came out of it; and even more beautiful girls on its banks.'

'Quite true,' said another, 'you've only got to look at me.'

'Or me,' said a third.

But Orpheus would not look at them. He went on weeping.

They began to get annoyed.

'Play another tune, Orpheus,' one of them said, 'everybody's sick of that noise. Even the sun has a headache.'

'Aren't we good enough for you?' another demanded.

'You're insulting us!'

'We're far prettier than Eurydice was.'

'And not half so silly!'

'Look at us, Orpheus!'

'Look at me!'

'And *me*!'

Orpheus shook his head and wept.

Losing their tempers, the Thracian maidens snatched his lute out of his hands and threw it into the river.

Orpheus went on weeping.

So they picked him up, tore him to pieces, and threw the bits into the river, too.

*

Poor Orpheus. Down the river his head floats, still singing wet songs. His lute floats beside him, and the rippling water plucks softly at its strings.

Fainter and fainter grows the sad singing.

All is quiet now. There is only the sighing of the rushes and the gentle sounds of the river weeping over its stones.

Happy Orpheus. He was taken down to the Underworld, where all the dead had to go in those far-away, long-ago days.

Eurydice was waiting for him. They ran into each other's arms. Their faces were so bright with love that they lit up Pluto's dark kingdom, showing the dust and the stained rocks and the rubbish pushed into corners.

Pluto, shading his eyes from the unaccustomed glare, said irritably, 'Oh, go away, Orpheus. Run along and play in the Elysian fields. And take your girl with you.'

So now they walk happily hand in hand through the fields, singing such pretty love songs together, that the grey ghosts clap their silent hands, and smile with remembered joy.

Or so some people say.

Second-best Boy

It's a shock to find that you dislike your best friend. Positively hate her. There she sat on the other side of the café table, sipping a strawberry milkshake, and shining. Trust her to hog the only patch of sunlight that managed to struggle through the dirty window.

They had met over five years ago, when they were both new and a little lost in the hurly-burly of the Comprehensive.

'Do you know anyone here?' Cathy had asked.

'No,' Rebecca said.

'Nor do I. I'm Cathy Sharwood. Let's be friends.'

And they had been friends, true friends, equals, Rebecca thought sadly, until . . . when had it happened?

When had Cathy changed from a fat, cheerful carrot-top into this flower-garden of a girl, with her bright marigold hair, eyes like dark, wet pansies and a mouth like a blooming rose? This honeyed boy-trap, this pretty hypocrite.

She even smelled of flowers now, though that came out of a bottle labelled 'Geranium Girl'. A cheap scent, Rebecca thought, sniffing. And she longed for the old Cathy, who had smelled of soap and peppermint, and whose feet, newly released from hot running-shoes, stank like everybody else's.

'But you must come, you must,' Cathy was saying now, opening her eyes very wide – as if they were not large enough already. The milkshake had left a soft froth, like pink cuckoo spit, on her rosy mouth. 'I said you would. Jonathan's got his dad's car, and he's bringing a friend . . .'

A friend? Forgotten his name, have you? That figures, Rebecca thought bitterly. She'd made up foursomes with Cathy before and she knew that the extra boy would be eminently forgettable. Whether fat and greasy or thin and earnest, he would certainly be both dull and resentful, as unwilling to accept second-best as she was herself.

In the mirror behind Cathy's head, Rebecca saw her own face reflected dimly, like a faded watercolour.

Nothing wrong with it. On a good day, she sometimes thought it looked quite pretty. But beside Cathy's glowing face, it appeared washed out, as if her own subtle colours had been drained away to add to the gaudy splendour of her friend.

'Becky, what's the matter?' Cathy asked, her soft eyes looking almost convincingly innocent and bewildered. 'I thought you'd be pleased. Don't you like Jonathan Drake?'

Bitch, Rebecca thought. Don't pretend you don't know. Don't tell me you've never noticed how I blush whenever I see him. Don't tell me you've never noticed how I gulp and stammer if he asks me the time or what's on at the local cinema. Once he rested his hand on my shoulder and I trembled so much that you asked me, in front of him, if I was sickening for something. I could have killed you.

I never washed that blouse. The imprint of his hand is still on it, folded away in a plastic bag and hidden in my wardrobe. How you'd laugh if you knew. You wouldn't understand, would you? Shakespeare would. Dante would. All the great poets would understand. I love Jonathan Drake. I've loved him for over a year and I know he'll never notice me. Why should he? All the girls at school are in love with him. Except you. You only want his scalp to add to your collection, another heart to hang on that charm bracelet you keep jangling in front of my nose.

Rebecca did not, of course, say any of this aloud.

'Jonathan?' she asked, trying to sound uninterested. 'He's all right, I suppose. Bit conceited.'

'You can't really blame him. I mean, he's very good-looking. Don't you think so, Becky? Madge Hempson says he looks like a Greek god. Though I always thought Greeks were supposed to be dark, and he's so fair. Perhaps she meant a statue. Come to think of it, he is a bit like that photograph of the Apollo statue you've got hanging over your bed.'

'Is he? Can't say I've noticed,' Rebecca lied.

Why are you doing this to me, Cathy? she wondered silently. What have I done to make you want to hurt me? Is it because I got better exam results than you did? Or because I was chosen to be Juliet in the end-of-term play? Or does it go further back, to our first year at Braeside, when my drawing was pinned up on the art room wall and yours wasn't? Have you secretly resented me all these years?

'Please say you'll come, Becky,' Cathy said. 'It won't be the same without you. We've always done everything together . . .'

They had. Swimming together in the summer river, skating on the winter ice, eating peanuts side by side in the cheapest seats of the cinema, cycling over the switch-back hills. Once the brakes on Rebecca's bicycle had gone and she'd hurtled down the hill helplessly towards the crossroads at the bottom. She'd survived then, with only a grazed knee and a buckled front wheel. Now she felt she was hurtling down a hill again, leaving her childhood far behind her, lost for ever. Her very memories were spoilt. It was like finding a maggot in an apple core: the taste of those years, once sweet, now made her want to vomit.

'Jonathan's calling for us at eight,' Cathy went on, taking her silence, if not for agreement, at least for a sign of weakening. 'You'll have plenty of time to wash your hair. We thought of driving out to that new place by the river. You know, The Green Willow. They say it's super. The food's good and there's a disco, and a riverside walk with coloured lights in the trees. And plenty of shadows, too,' she added with a little giggle that called up pictures of kisses in the dark. Cathy and Jonathan . . .

'I feel sick,' Rebecca said, 'in the back of a car.'

'You can sit in the front. I don't mind.'

Rebecca stared at her. 'Who's driving, then?' she asked.

'Jonathan. It's his dad's car,' Cathy told her, her face as innocent as an angel's. 'I'll sit in the back with his friend.'

What was she up to? Was she so damn sure of

Jonathan that she could condescend to be generous to her poor, lovesick friend? Just for half an hour's drive before she beckoned him away.

Oh Lord, thought Rebecca. Let me beat her at her own game. She stared hopelessly into the mirror. Eight o'clock. Plenty of time before then to have her hair dyed red, yellow or black, to have it cut short or brushed out into a flaming bush. Perhaps her mother would lend her the money to buy a new outfit: tight satin trousers or a swirling skirt. What did Jonathan like?

What he liked was sitting in front of her in a faded cotton dress from Marks and Spencers, with no need for make-up on her flower face, no hair dye to dull the glowing lustre of her red-gold hair. No need for false eyelashes or fingernails, no padded bras to push her out or tight belts to hold her in. Cathy's puppy fat had all gone. She was a fully-grown bitch.

'We'll have fun, won't we?' she said.

'Yes,' Rebecca agreed, and thought about pushing her best friend into the river.

At seven o'clock that evening, Rebecca sat in front of her mirror, brushing her newly-washed hair. She had not had it dyed, nor had she bought anything new to wear. Why waste her money? Even if she had her hair dyed green, Jonathan probably would not notice.

Her mother would. Her mother noticed everything: a new lipstick, a pair of high-heeled shoes, a red silk shirt. Ever since Rebecca was fifteen, her mother had been watching her closely, dreading the day when her daughter would bring home a hideously unsuitable boyfriend, with long greasy hair and his shirt open to his navel.

'Where are you going this evening?' she'd ask, eyeing Rebecca's tight black trousers uneasily.

'To the cinema.'

'Who with?'

'Some friends from school.'

'Anyone I know?'

'Cathy, Sue, William – just the usual lot. No one in particular,' Rebecca would say, not mentioning Jonathan with whom she was already in love.

'Have a nice time, darling,' her mother would say, relieved.

Now that Rebecca was nearly seventeen, however, her mother's worries had changed.

'You're looking pretty tonight. Are you going out with anyone special?' she'd ask hopefully.

'Just Cathy.'

'Cathy's looking very glamorous nowadays, I must say. Has she got a boyfriend yet?'

'Yes. Several.'

'Oh well, there's safety in numbers,' her mother

would say. 'Don't worry. You're very young still. Plenty of time to think of boyfriends when you've finished your exams. I'm glad you're so sensible.'

But her eyes would inspect Rebecca uneasily, as if wondering if there was anything wrong with this daughter who gave her no trouble; who never came home at three in the morning, or painted the walls of her bedroom black and purple, or flounced out of the house in a screaming tantrum, vowing never to return. Who was so unlike the daughters of all her friends.

Poor Mum, Rebecca thought. It must be boring for her to have nothing to complain about at her coffee mornings. Perhaps I should have dyed my hair green for her sake – 'You'll never guess what Rebecca did! I could've screamed when I saw her. Her hair! Bright green!'

She smiled ruefully at her reflection. It was too late now. Light-brown hair, pale skin, hazel eyes. The face of a quiet, well-brought-up girl – as dull at ditchwater. Oh well, it was fitting. A second-best girl for a second-best boy. She wondered without much interest what he would be like. One thing you could bet on. He'd have spots.

He did. His name was Peter Swithen, and he had three ripe red spots on his chin. Otherwise he was unremarkable, of average height, skinny, with untidy dark hair, two strands of which hung over his spectacles like windscreen wipers. His eyes were on the small side but at least they looked at Rebecca when he was introduced to her, without showing any obvious sign of disappointment. Perhaps, she thought, he had expected worse.

She had had no faith in Cathy's promise that she could sit in the front seat of the car. She'd been sure that at the last moment Cathy would find a good reason why she herself should sit there. Rebecca was so astonished when Cathy climbed into the back without protest that she stood stupidly on the pavement, staring at the empty seat beside Jonathan.

'Come on,' he said. 'Or don't you trust my driving?'

She got in beside him, blushing and tongue-tied. She could think of nothing to say. She dared not even look at him for fear of seeing boredom or impatience on his face. Wishing she had never come, she sat stiffly in her seat, her elbows pressed tight against her sides, staring blindly in front of her as he drove through the outskirts of the little town. In the back seat, Cathy and Peter were whispering together, and she heard Cathy giggle.

Her cheeks flamed. She was sure that they were laughing at her. It would amuse Cathy to betray her secret to Peter. Oh Lord, had she told Jonathan as well? It was horribly easy to imagine. Perhaps she had said, 'Poor old Becky, she's hopelessly gone on you. You must've noticed,

Johnny. She turns bright pink whenever she sees you. It's pathetic. You should've seen her face when I said she could sit next to you in the car. You don't mind, do you, Johnny? It's only till we get to The Green Willow, then we'll change partners.'

I hate her, Rebecca thought. Staring through the windscreen, she saw before her not the narrow winding road but a wide, shallow river, thick with mud and filth. She saw her best friend wallowing oozily out of it, her bright hair dimmed by a crown of scum . . .

And won't I laugh, she thought vindictively.

'. . . don't you agree?' Jonathan asked.

'Yes,' she said uneasily, having no idea what he'd been talking about.

'I wish Dad would get a new one,' he went on. 'This old rattle box has just about had it. And it's false economy, as I keep telling him. Everyone knows you should trade in a car every . . .'

Cathy giggled in the back again and the extra boy laughed. 'I don't believe you,' he said, 'you're making it up.' Then their voices sank to a low mumble again. Rebecca tried to turn round to glare at them, but the seat-belt and head-rest restricted her movements. All she got was a glimpse of two shadows sitting close together, and a crick in her neck.

'Do you know what I'd like?' Jonathan asked.

'No,' she replied truthfully, for she had not been listening to him, she was too busy trying to hear what they were saying behind her.

'A Range Rover,' he said. 'Does that surprise you?'

'Yes,' she replied. 'No. Perhaps.'

Fortunately he did not seem to expect her to take an intelligent part in his conversation, but went on to explain the reasons for his choice, talking with enthusiasm about engine capacity, speed ratio and petrol consumption.

'It's the four-wheel drive that appeals to me most,' he said.

'Yes. I can see that.'

'You can cross a desert in one, or go up a mountain –'

'A mountain?' Rebecca repeated blankly, for the countryside they were driving through was flat, with nothing higher than a hedge in sight.

'I don't mean Mount Everest, of course,' Jonathan said, taking his eyes off the road to smile at her briefly. 'But you could go quite a way up.'

'Yes, I suppose so.'

She must try and concentrate on what he was saying. This was Jonathan, whom she loved. And there she was, sitting beside him in the summer dusk, so close that their elbows nearly touched, and the air between them seemed to quiver. She turned her head and gazed admiringly at his profile. How beautiful he was, with the straight nose and rounded chin of an Apollo, and the close-fitting cap of dark-gold curls . . .

It's the happiest moment of my life, she told herself, or it would be, if only he'd shut up for a minute. I don't want to hear about cars. I want to hear what they're whispering about in the back. Cathy and the second-best boy. I bet they're planning to play some horrible joke on me.

She was wrong. They had no thought to spare for her, or for Jonathan, or for any of the chattering people at the little tables in the garden of The Green Willow. They did not look at them, but only at each other. Above their heads, a faded moon had risen and fairy lights flowered in the trees along the river bank. But nothing could outshine the brightness on their faces as they leaned together, eating chicken and chips out of the same basket. They were in love.

Good grief! Rebecca thought. What in Heaven's name can she see in *him*?

And she stared at Peter in astonishment, half-expecting him to have changed like the frog in a fairy story. But he looked just the same as he had before, skinny and spotty and utterly unremarkable.

Was it a joke? Were they just pretending, play-acting in order to make a fool of her. No, Rebecca thought, seeing her friend's face glow like a pale flower in the moonlight, turning towards the spotted boy as if he were the sun. She watched them wander off hand in hand down the riverside walk, with the fairy lights high up in the trees and the kissing shadows below.

'I'm sorry if I'm boring you,' Jonathan said stiffly.

'What?'

'You haven't been listening to a word I've said, have you?'

'Yes, I have,' she said, adding quickly, before he could ask her to repeat his last sentence. 'Have you known Peter long?'

'Peter Swithen?' he asked, as if the world was full of Peters and he didn't much care for any of them. 'Yes. Ages. He's my cousin.'

'Is he very brilliant, or something?'

'No, not particularly. He's clever, but no cleverer than –' he hesitated. She was sure he'd been going to say 'than me', but he changed it to 'Many other boys. Why?'

'I just wondered. Are his parents very rich?'

'Good Lord, no. His father's a teacher, and that's what he wants to be. Why all this interest in him? I must say it's rather the limit,' he added bitterly, 'when you ask a girl out, you don't expect her to do nothing but talk about your bloody cousin.'

'You didn't ask me. Cathy did,' Rebecca said, and smiled. She felt as if she had been given back the happy years of her childhood. There was no need to forget them now. Cathy had been a true friend all the time.

'Well, I knew you were coming,' Jonathan was saying. 'I mean, she asked you for me, didn't she? I can't see it makes any difference. I just don't understand you. I always thought you –' He broke off, with such a look of offended vanity on his face that she couldn't help laughing.

'You always thought I fancied you?' she asked mockingly; but then, seeing him flush and look hurt, she added kindly, 'Well, perhaps I do.'

As they walked hand in hand by the river, she glanced at him sideways. He was beautiful and clever, a little vain but you could hardly blame him for that. How odd of Cathy, she thought, to leave this treasure for me. Won't Mum be surprised when I bring him home. Won't all the other girls be sick with envy.

Yet she knew she would never feel for him again the same bitter-sweet adoration she had felt before. No longer would a single smile from him be enough to brighten a whole day. After all, if Cathy, who was so beautiful that she could have chosen any boy she wanted, had passed him over, it must mean that Jonathan was the second-best boy.

Rebecca was not certain whether to be glad or sorry. She had lost something. She did not belong any longer in the great company of tragic lovers, sighing for unattainable stars. This Romeo would be only too welcome at her house. He would probably talk to her father about cars . . .

But his hand in hers was warm and human. There was something to be said, she thought as she smiled at him, for second-best boys.

The Pram Lady

They walked in silence, partly because the hill was steep and it was hot, and partly because they had run out of things to say. They did not know each other very well. They'd only met last week at somebody's party, but already William was beginning to wonder whether he was in love.

Somehow it made conversation difficult. He wanted to impress her but his head felt hot and stupid. His mouth filled with saliva so that he had to keep swallowing, and his voice, when he did speak, sounded thick and strange. Either it was love or he was sickening for something.

The girl walked quietly by his side. Her face had lost its earlier animation, and looked sad and remote. Perhaps she was bored.

When they were halfway up the hill an extraordinary figure, wheeling a battered, old-fashioned pram, came out of a side-turning and crossed the road in front of them. She, for it was some sort of woman, was enormously fat. Her head was covered by an ancient and unravelling straw hat, around which were attached a few crumpled and faded red silk roses. From beneath the brim, streaky grey hair draggled on her shoulders. She was wearing a man's tweed jacket, liberally splattered by stains of every colour. A purple skirt, also stained, reached nearly to her bare ankles. Her large and grubby feet were in thonged sandals. The pram, as far as he could see, for she was walking away from them at a surprisingly rapid pace, was filled not with a baby but with jumble.

'God, what a fright, what a ridiculous creature,' William said, nudging the girl beside him. 'Whatever can it be?'

'It,' the girl said coldly, 'is my mother.'

He laughed, not believing her, for the woman, though he had hardly seen her face in the shadow of the straw hat, had nevertheless seemed far too old to be the mother of a sixteen-year-old girl. Nor could he believe that a girl like Helena, so beautiful, so cool and clean with her shining brown hair and her pale-green dress, could have any connection with that dreadful old bag woman.

'Some mother!' he said, grinning, and saw too late the anger and contempt in her eyes.

'I never want to see you again!' she shouted, and turning, went running down the hill.

After a stunned moment, he raced after her, caught her up, began to apologise breathlessly – what could he say? He didn't know. He could only stammer:

'I – didn't mean . . . I'm sorry . . . I didn't mean that woman, that lady – I meant – it was a dog! Didn't you see that funny dog? That's what I was talking about . . .'

But his lies were no good. 'There was no dog,' she said angrily and walked on. When he caught her by the arm, she told him to let go or she'd scream. He should have believed her because she carried out her threat, opening her mouth wide and screaming loudly. People looked over their garden walls, came out of houses, opened their windows. He was forced to let her go. She ran across the road, jumped on to a bus and was carried out of sight.

Helena Banks, having travelled the short distance home by bus and not by foot, arrived there ten minutes before her mother, and lay in wait. As soon as she heard the front door open and the squeaky bump of the pram wheels over the threshold, she ran out into the hall.

'You've done it! You've done it again!' she shouted furiously. 'I could kill you!'

'I hoped you hadn't noticed me,' her mother said sheepishly. 'I'm sorry, dear. But I thought you said you were going up to town. I thought I was safe.'

'We changed our minds.'

'I'm sorry,' her mother said again. She wheeled the pram through the hall and into her workroom at the back of the house. Helena followed her, grabbed her by the shoulders and swivelled her round, forcing her mother to confront her own reflection in the large studio mirror.

'Look at yourself! Don't you look disgusting? That horrible hat!' She snatched if off her mother's head, tried to tear it with her hands but, finding the straw tougher than it looked, threw it on the floor and stamped on it.

'I got it at the scouts' jumble sale for five pence,' her mother said wistfully. 'I thought the roses were a pretty colour. I didn't mean to wear it. I thought I might use it in a still life one day. But I couldn't find my white hat this morning. The sun was so bright, I needed something to shield my eyes. You haven't seen my white hat anywhere, have you?'

'If you mean that thing I threw in the dustbin last week,' Helena said, 'it wasn't white. It hasn't been white for years.'

Her mother sighed, took a canvas carefully out of the pram and put it on the easel by the window. It was a painting of some boys fishing in one of the Highgate ponds, bold and splashy – you cold feel the sun was hot and the water wet. Helena liked her mother's paintings but would have sacrificed them all to have a more ordinary mother, one who would pass in a crowd without heads turning to stare, elbows nudging – 'God, what a fright!'

Her friends' mothers who painted didn't go around looking like bag women. They wore pretty, flowered smocks, kept their paints in neat satchels and their fingernails clean.

'Bunch of amateurs,' her mother had snorted when Helena had pointed this out.

'Mark's father is a professional and he doesn't look like a discarded paint rag tied round a pudding –'

'He does abstracts. Never has to set foot outside when he's working, so how do you know what he looks like then? He may paint in the nude, for all you know. That's one way of keeping your clothes clean. Perhaps I should try it.'

The idea of her fat mother painting in the nude had made Helena laugh. But she didn't feel like laughing now. She had liked William better than anyone else. She hadn't wanted to lose him. Ever since she had started at the sixth-form college she had made new friends only to lose them again; sometimes in a few days, sometimes after weeks, but always sooner or later they had seen her mother wheeling her terrible pram and had laughed. 'Hey, just look at that old fright.'

And that was that. All over. The end. Helena never wanted to see them again, refused their telephone calls, tore up their letters, walked past them, stony-faced, in the corridors or in the streets outside the college.

She never warned them. Never said, as she might have done, 'My mother's a painter. She's a bit eccentric, so if you see a large woman in peculiar clothes wheeling a pram full of easels and canvases and rags through the streets of Highgate, it'll just be my mother going out to work. Don't laugh. I never forgive people who laugh at my mother. I'm the only person who's allowed to do that.'

Sometimes she felt more like crying.

She watched her mother washing her brushes at the sink in the corner of the workroom, first in white spirit and then in soap and water, carefully, paying more attention to them than she ever did to herself.

'Why don't you wash your own hair while you're about it?' Helena asked. 'It's horrible. You're not young any more. Grey hair looks awful when it's long.'

'It's not grey,' her mother protested, glancing sideways at the mirror. 'At least, not all of it. Perhaps I should have it dyed.'

'No. Have it cut short. And permed.'

'Then I'd look like every other ageing woman. But

that's what you want, isn't it, Helena? An ordinary mother like your friends have. You're very conventional. It's not your fault. You take after your father. That's all he wanted, a wallpaper wife, something decorative but quiet in the background that he didn't have to listen to. It was the beginning of my real life when he walked out. I felt like cheering.'

'Will you cheer when I walk out?' Helena asked, and saw the sudden fear in her mother's eyes.

'Helena –'

But Helena left the room, slamming the door behind her.

She ran up to her bedroom and thought about packing. She could go to her father. It wasn't his day for her but that didn't matter. He and Nicole had often said, 'You know you're welcome here any time, Helena.'

She liked her father's second wife well enough, liked their neat, comfortable home. She could have gone to live with them permanently, they'd said so, but she'd always refused. She couldn't walk out and leave her mother, like Dad had done. Not that she blamed him, but if she walked out too, her mother would be alone. There'd be no one to look after her, to stop her from eating all the time; meat pies and crisps, cream doughnuts and Danish pastries, and bags of chocolate fudge wedged among the tubes of paint in her workroom, the paper smudged with blue and green and red from her fingers. No one to throw away her crazy hats when they became too dirty. No one to remind her to have her hair cut.

Helena could manage to do without boyfriends, but she did not think her mother could do without her.

When William had watched the bus carrying Helena away, he had told himself he was well out of that one. The little bitch! That awful mother! He laughed out loud, trying to convince himself – and anyone who was staring at him – that he didn't care that she'd ditched him. There were plenty more girls in the sea – and he hoped they'd all drown.

But that night he couldn't sleep for thinking about Helena. He saw again the anger and contempt in her eyes when she'd said she never wanted to see him again; and hid his face in shame, remembering how he'd nudged her in the ribs and giggled and called her poor old mother a fright. How could he have been so heartless, so vulgar? He, who prided himself on his compassion for the whole world, who ran in marathons for charity, gave ten per cent of his pocket money to Oxfam, how could he have insulted a woman just because she was poor and peculiar?

Would Helena ever forgive him? She must, she must, he thought, turning and tossing on his moonlit bed. He'd apologise tomorrow at college. He'd take her flowers from the garden.

But Helena would not listen to his apologies. She threw his flowers on the floor and ran off. When he cornered her by the library, she put her fingers in her ears and threatened to scream again if he didn't go away. He did not doubt that she would. She was amazing. He'd never met a girl like her before. But then he'd never been in love.

He was a stubborn boy. He refused to give up. He wrote her letters at college but she tore them up and sent them back to him. He followed her home and she threatened to call a policeman and complain that he was molesting her.

'I'm not. I just want to say I'm sorry.'

'All right, you've said it. Now go away.'

'Will you forgive me?'

'No.'

'I'll never stop saying sorry until you do.'

'God, what a bore you are!' she shouted, and ran into the house, slamming the door in his face when he tried to follow. Looking out of the net curtains in the living-room, she saw him standing gazing up at the house. She thought he looked surprised. Had he expected them to live in cardboard boxes? Probably. He'd obviously taken her mother for a tramp.

'Isn't that the boy I saw you with last week?' her mother asked, joining her at the window.

'Yes.'

'He looks nice.'

'He's a pest. He won't leave me alone.'

'You're lucky,' her mother said. 'I wouldn't want a boy like that to leave me alone, if I was your age.'

'I hate him,' Helena said. She flung open the window at the bottom and shouted it aloud. 'Go away! I hate you! I hate you!'

William looked at her sadly for a moment, then he turned and walked off.

'Now you've driven him away,' her mother said. 'Poor young man. He looked so nice. I hope you don't come to regret it.'

'You wouldn't think he was so nice if you knew what he'd said about you.'

'What was that?'

Helena told her.

'I don't suppose he knew I was your mother,' Mrs Banks said generously. 'You oughtn't to hold it against him. You've called me worse things than that and I've always forgiven you.'

'That's different. I'm your daughter,' said Helena, and then added slowly, 'besides, I understand. I know why you've let yourself go like this. It's because of Dad, isn't it? You don't care what you look like any more since Dad left. You've given up.'

'Oh, Helena!' Mrs Banks said, half laughing, half ashamed. 'You've forgotten. I've always been fat and untidy. Don't you remember how it got on your poor father's nerves? I expect that was partly why we broke up. We just weren't suited. He was always so neat and so particular, and as for me –' She walked over to the mirror and regarded her reflection critically. 'You know, I really don't care what I look like, but it's not fair on you, is it? Or on the unfortunate young men who laugh at me, not knowing I'm your mother. Why don't you laugh with them, Helena? I won't mind.' She smiled. 'My shoulders are broad enough.'

'I can't,' Helena said. 'I hate it. I won't have them laughing at you.'

Her mother looked at her. 'I'll start dieting tomorrow,' she promised. 'It'll be good for me. And I'll have my hair cut and curled. Poor Helena, I'll do my best not to shame you in front of your next boyfriend.'

'It doesn't matter,' Helena said. 'I don't want any more boyfriends.'

Her mother raised her eyebrows thoughtfully, but did not say anything.

Helena did not see William again that term. He was not at college the next day or for the rest of the week before they broke up for the holidays. She'd have liked to have asked his friends where he was, but she was afraid they'd tell him. She wished her mother would ask about him, if only to hear his name again, but her mother was busy painting, making use of the long, light evenings to get ready for an exhibition.

Oddly, now that William was gone, Helena was haunted by him. She seemed to see him everywhere out of the corner of her eyes, but when she looked round, he was not there. Her mind was filled with images of him. Sometimes she seemed to hear his voice. She began to dream of him at night, dreams dominated by the tall, thin, unhappy figure. Sometimes he was in a street market, sometimes walking down a shabby street, once he crouched in an empty field with his hands over his eyes – but always there was a sense of bleak misery about him that made her wake up shivering. She began to wonder if he was dead.

At last she could bear it no longer. She went into her mother's workroom and said, 'Mum, do you remember William Rendell? The boy I shouted at? The one you said looked nice?'

'Yes, I do. I remember him well.'

'I'm a bit worried about him. He wasn't at college for the last week and I haven't seen him anywhere. I wondered if he was ill.'

Her mother didn't say anything. She was looking at

her painting, her eyes narrowed. Helena glanced at it. Her mother had painted a group of cyclists on what appeared to be a large, otherwise empty, concrete playground. The bicycle wheels, set at different angles, made an abstract pattern, echoed and somehow made sinister by the distorted shadows on the concrete. On the left side there was a solitary cyclist, a tall, thin youth with drooping shoulders, who watched the others with the sad air of an outcast.

'That looks a bit like William,' Helena said.

Her mother did not answer. Helena, glancing quickly at her, caught the tail of a disappearing smile on her face. She stared back at the painting, and then at the completed canvases hanging on the walls of the workroom. They were all figure compositions; people in street markets, sitting in trains, walking along deserted roads, standing waiting on windy railway platforms – and in every one, sometimes in the foreground, sometimes half hidden in a corner, was the figure of a dejected youth, thin and tall, with untidy dark hair and sad eyes. William Rendell.

'He came to see me one day when you were at college,' her mother said. 'Such a nice boy. He brought me some red roses and told me what had happened, how you'd quarrelled because he'd been rude about me. He was very upset, very ashamed of himself, poor boy, and really, as I told him, it wasn't his fault. It was mine for going about looking such a guy. I have been dieting, Helena. I've already lost six pounds – not that it shows yet, a mere drop in the ocean. William offered to sit for me for nothing, to make amends, he said. I think he really hoped to see you. However, I'm not one to turn my nose up at a free model. He was very useful.' She waved her hands at the paintings on the wall. 'Very patient. I'm doing a portrait of him for his mother.' She took the cyclist off the easel and put another canvas in its place.

'What do you think of that?' she asked.

The painted William sprawled on the studio chair. His glossy eyes looked straight out of the canvas into hers. His painted mouth turned up in a hopeful smile. He did not look sad any more. He looked pleased with himself, like a cat who's found a comfortable home at last and hopes it will be allowed to stay.

'He's coming for the last sitting this afternoon,' her mother said. 'He should be here any minute. I suppose you wouldn't stay in and make us all tea, would you, darling?'

It had been a plot, Helena thought, looking round at all the painted Williams. She'd been brainwashed. They'd been in it together, William and her mother, that was obvious. But she couldn't help laughing.

'Oh, all right,' she said. 'I'll make tea for you both. But you're not to have any cake. Me and William will eat it all.'

Cinderella Girl

Bella Jones didn't like Meg Hunter one little bit. She was too rough, too noisy and too grubby.

'It's not only the way she crashes about, knocking things over,' she said. 'It's everything about her. She always looks such a fright. That great bush of hair, I bet she never combs it. And her face is often *dirty*. As for her clothes! She came to school yesterday with those horrible green trousers of hers done up with safety pins, did you notice? She just doesn't care what she looks like. She's an utter mess.'

It was true. Edward had to admit it. Yet there was something he liked about Meg, a sort of warm glow, a friendliness. She laughed a lot. The smaller kids loved her.

Meg was young for her age, that was the trouble, a big untidy girl with shaggy brown hair, like an overgrown puppy. She still climbed the trees on the common and rolled down the steep grass bank as he had done when he was a kid. He even saw her playing football with the boys from their old primary school, and had been tempted for a moment to join in. But the ground was wet and muddy, and he was wearing his new trousers. Also his mother was with him.

His mother liked people to look nice. 'It only takes a little effort to look clean and tidy,' she was fond of telling Edward, 'and it makes all the difference to what people think of you. Always remember that, Edward.' He knew she didn't approve of Meg. She never said so outright, but he could tell. Her plucked eyebrows always rose when she saw her, and she'd shake her head, as if to say, 'Well, really!'

'Isn't that Meg Hunter over there, playing football with those boys?' she'd asked. 'Covered in mud, poor girl. Just look at her! It's odd because her mother is really very nice, you know. And the two older girls are always beautifully dressed. You'd never take them for the same family. I wonder Mrs Hunter lets Meg go around looking like that.'

'She's Meg's stepmother,' Edward told her.

'It's not always easy being a stepmother,' his mother said. 'I imagine Meg can be quite a handful.'

A Cinderella girl, Edward thought. Poor Meg, nobody cares what she looks like. Perhaps her stepmother grudges every penny she has to spend on her, and won't buy her new clothes or even a hairbrush, so that she has to use safety pins when her zips break and comb her hair with her fingers.

'She's in your class, isn't she?' his mother asked.

'Yes.'

'Is she clever?'

'I don't know,' Edward said. 'I've never noticed.'

His mother laughed. 'I don't suppose you have,' she said. 'She's not the sort of girl boys look at.'

His mother didn't know everything, however. Edward did look at Meg, quite often. He wasn't certain why. She was plump and her clothes never seemed to fit her and she had big feet. On Sundays, however, when they met by chance in the park, they'd stay together, talking or watching their local team play football. He always looked forward to seeing her.

But it was Bella he really wanted to date. Pretty popular Bella whom a lot of boys claimed would let you kiss her in the cinema or in the bushes behind the cycle shed. He had never kissed a girl, not properly, and was beginning to feel left out. Of course they might be only boasting.

'Have you ever kissed a girl?' he asked his best friend

Michael, who was tall and skinny and clever, and could be trusted not to betray him.

'Of course I have! Millions of times. Can't get away from them,' Michael told him. 'They swarm over me every Christmas. Mum's only got to put up a bit of mistletoe and I have to hide to avoid being trampled on.'

'No, seriously, have you?'

'My lips are sealed,' Michael said grandly. 'I'm not one to kiss and tell.'

'I'm not asking for names. Just a straight answer, yes or no.'

'No. What about you.'

'No,' Edward admitted, 'but don't tell anybody.'

Michael laughed. 'Don't sound so sad. We're still young. Far too young, my mum would say. Do you want to kiss just any girl, or one in particular?'

'I want to kiss Bella Jones.'

'Oh, her! I might've guessed. You always want to do what other people do,' Michael said. He was not one of Bella's admirers. 'Well, why don't you?'

He made it sound easy. Full of hope, Edward had asked Bella to come to see a film with him.

'No, I don't think so,' she said.

'Why not?' he asked. 'I thought you liked me.'

'Whatever gave you that idea?' she said.

'Oh, come on! There's a good film on at the Odeon. *Alligator Angel*. I'll treat you. What about tomorrow?'

She shook her head. 'Not tomorrow.'

'Wednesday?'

'Sorry. Can't manage Wednesday.'

'What about Thursday, then?'

'I dunno. I might. I'll think about it,' she said.

On Thursday morning, he came to school early, in his new trousers and his best shirt. But when Bella came, she told him she was going out with Kevin Clarke.

'But you promised –'

'I never promised. I just said I might,' she told him. 'Ask me again some time.'

So he asked her the next day, and the next day and the next, and every time she said, 'I dunno. I might. Ask me again.'

The last time she said this, he turned away without a word, and went to look out of the window, ignoring her. She didn't like that.

'What are you looking at?' she asked, coming to stand beside him.

'Nothing in particular.'

'Yes, you are. You're looking at Meg Hunter. Here she comes, late as usual. Doesn't she look stupid when she runs? Look at that smudge on her face! She can't have washed at all this morning.

Edward knew how Meg got smudges on her face. Sometimes, when he was late, he saw her going along the road in front of him, trailing her fingers over the ledges of the buildings, stroking the dusty plastic dog outside the pet shop, then pushing her unruly hair back from her face with sooty hands.

'It's only dust,' he said.

'And what on earth does she think she's wearing? That cardigan's hideous! And it's coming unravelled at the sleeve. Why doesn't she make her stepmother buy her some decent clothes.'

'What she needs is a fairy godmother, a pumpkin and a prince,' Edward said.

'What she needs is a hot bath and a haircut,' Bella retorted, wrinkling her pretty little nose. 'Don't tell me you fancy her, Edward?'

Before he could answer, Mr Dunlock, their teacher, came into the room and ordered them to their places. Edward saw Meg, trying to slip unnoticed into the room, trip over someone's leg – whose? Was it Bella's? – and stumble heavily against one of the tables.

'Late again, Meg?' Mr Dunlock said. He peered at her through his spectacles. 'What's that on your face? It looks like soot. Go and wash it off, there's a good girl.'

As Meg left the room, some of the girls giggled and whispered. Edward was too far away to see who they were. He wondered if Bella was one of them. She could be spiteful, he'd already found that out, but he didn't want to have to start again with another girl. He was used to being in love with her, used to asking her out, even used to being refused.

There was something to be said for unrequited love. It was safer. Often, in his sleep, when he tried to kiss Bella, he tripped over his own feet and missed her altogether. Once he dreamed he was sitting next to her in the dark cinema, holding her hand. But when he leaned over to kiss her, she suddenly turned into Mrs Trenter, their head teacher, who shouted angrily, 'Edward Walden, you've failed your tests! What will your mother say?'

Nevertheless it hurt his pride that Bella should keep on refusing him when she went out with several other boys who were not, he considered, better looking or more amusing or in any way nicer than he was.

'I don't mean to be conceited, but honestly!' he said to his friend Michael. 'She's been out with Kevin a lot, and he's the dregs. Why do you think it is?'

'The girl's daft,' Michael said kindly. 'She's got bad taste.'

The next Sunday, Edward walked moodily in the park, looking for Meg. He found her sitting in her favourite tree and climbed up beside her.

'Do you think there's something wrong with me?' he asked.

'In what way? Have you got a pain or spots or something?'

'No, I meant . . . Am I off-putting in any way? Have I got halitosis or do my feet stink?'

'No,' she said.

'If you were Bella, would you rather go out with me or Kevin Clarke?'

Meg laughed. 'Kevin Clarke writes her poems,' she said.

'Poems?' Edward repeated in astonishment. 'Whatever for?'

'She likes them. She sticks them in an album opposite photographs of herself, and shows them to us.'

'Good grief,' Edward said, appalled by this new slant on his beloved. 'What are they about?'

'They're all about her, of course,' Meg told him. 'You know the sort of thing:

> 'Oh, Bella's hair is brighter than the sun,
> And Bella's eyes are bluer than the sky –'

'What rot!' Edward said in disgust. 'It's not even true. Bella's hair is pretty enough but I bet it's never ripened any tomatoes. I wonder she can stomach such tripe. She must be terribly vain.'

Meg didn't say anything.

'*You* wouldn't want anyone to write poems to you, would you, Meg?' he asked.

'I don't know. Just once, perhaps. But nobody ever will,' she said. He thought she sounded a bit wistful.

'I'll write you a poem, if you like,' he offered. 'Not that I'm any good at it, but I bet I can do as well as Kevin. Shall I?'

'Don't say that my hair will ripen tomatoes because it won't,' she said, pushing it back from her face and leaving a smudge on her nose. 'It might do to plant mustard and cress in. Mum's always trying to persuade me to have it cut.'

'I shall be strictly truthful,' he promised.

'Oh dear.'

After a moment, he began:

> 'Your hair is rough and long and needs a cut,
> Your eyes are . . .'

'What colour are your eyes, Meg? I can't remember. Look at me, please?'

She turned her head. Her eyes were a greenish hazel and very bright. They reminded him of the sea at Cosheston, sparkling over the pebbles in the sunlight . . .

'Your mermaid eyes are flecked with gold
and green.
Your nose is smudged, your sleeve
unravelled but
Of all the girls at school you are my queen.'

He shouldn't have said that last line. It wasn't true, was it? What about Bella? Besides, he couldn't date Meg. His mother would have a fit and everybody at school would tease him. He looked at her anxiously, hoping she wouldn't take it seriously, but she only laughed and told him it was a splendid poem, far better than any of Kevin's.

'Don't worry,' she said. 'I won't tell Bella.'

At the end of term, their school had a summer disco in the assembly hall. Edward didn't think he'd go. He had given up asking Bella to come out with him, and no longer dreamed of her at night. So he was surprised when she came up to him and said, 'Aren't you going to ask if you can take me to the summer disco, Edward?'

'You don't need anyone to go with. You can just go,' he told her.

'I know that,' she said. 'I just thought you might want to call for me so we could go together.'

He looked at her suspiciously. 'Would you come with me if I asked you?'

'I dunno. I might,' she said and ran off, giggling.

'And I might ask some other girl,' he said, and walked off. He knew whom he was going to ask. It was only when he found Meg in the library that it occurred to him that she might refuse.

'Please,' he asked, as she hesitated.

'I thought you'd ask Bella Jones,' she said.

'No. I'm asking you.'

'I can't dance,' she said. 'I've never been to a disco.'

'Nor have I,' he told her and they smiled at one another.

He was nervous, standing outside the school on the Saturday of the party. Sometimes he was afraid Meg would not come after all, and Bella would laugh. Sometimes he was afraid Meg would come in her old green trousers, still done up with a safety-pin, with her hair unbrushed and her face smudged, and Bella would laugh even louder. Bella had arrived with Kevin Clarke, and they were waiting in the entrance, looking at him and sniggering; Bella with her yellow hair frizzed out and her claws sharpened.

'Who are you waiting for, Edward?' she called out, but just then a big silver car drew up outside the school gates, and a girl in a sea-green dress got out. Her long brown hair was sleek and shining, earrings sparkled in her ears and there were silver buckles on her shoes. As she walked towards them, the thin material of her dress swirled out like the waves of the sea.

Everyone stared.

'Meg,' Edward said, coming forward. 'Meg, you look fabulous.'

'Don't I look posh? I hardly know myself,' she told him, laughing. 'Mum and my sisters took me in hand. They've been longing to do it for ages, but I wouldn't let them. Mum's bought me a whole lot of new clothes, Josie gave me these earrings and Netta these bracelets.'

She was no Cinderella, after all. She was Meg, whose family loved her, enough to let her play football in the park and climb trees when she wanted to, and to do her proud when the time came. She's beautiful, he thought, and felt for a moment an odd pang of loss. Had she gone for good, the laughing, untidy, romping girl who'd not wanted to grow up?

'Don't change too much,' he said. Then, as she looked up at him, he noticed a small smudge of eyeblack on her left cheek. Without thinking, he bent down and kissed her, forgetting that Bella and her friends were watching until he heard the catcalls. He didn't care what they thought, not now. It was as if the kiss had broken a spell and set him free. Nobody was going to tell him what to think any longer, nor choose his friends for him. This was the girl he had always liked. The others could suit themselves.

A Proper Boy

Harry's father was a strong man, tall and muscular. He did exercises in front of an open window every morning and when he finished, he slapped his flat stomach four times. Hard. In summer, when Harry's own window was open, he could hear the sound very plainly. The last slap was always the loudest. Harry thought it was meant for him.

His father's name was Victor George Wellington. He had always wanted a son. A son to take to football matches, a son to play cricket with on the beach, to take sailing in small boats, and riding on large horses. He wanted a boy like his brother's son, Marcus, tough, rosy-cheeked, afraid of nothing. It was just his bad luck that he had four daughters, one after another. Victoria, Georgina,

Julie and Nell. He was fond of them, of course he was. He was not an ogre. He didn't say, 'Oh no! Not another girl,' when he saw them appear. But everyone knew he had wanted a son.

Harry's mother Isobel wasn't bothered. She thought the girls were fine and didn't want to have another child.

'Babies are tiring,' she told her husband. 'You wouldn't know that, Victor. You've always gone out to work. Going out to work is a rest cure compared to looking after babies and toddlers. I know. I've done both in my time. Besides the world is overpopulated. Four children are enough.'

Victor George Wellington didn't shout at her. He didn't insist. He just looked grave and disappointed, and went on looking disappointed, day after day, week after week, until in the end, she sighed and said, 'Oh, all right, Victor. One more child. One last chance for a boy.'

It was Harry's bad luck that he was that boy.

His sisters, Vicky, Georgie, Julie and Nell were tall, healthy girls with pink cheeks and bright eyes. Vicky was good at all games. Georgie had a silver medal for swimming, and Julie was a gymnast. Nell, the youngest and softest of his sisters, had recently abandoned her dolls for a cricket bat and a toy gun. Even his mother, though only of average height, was sturdy and strong. But Harry?

To be honest, Harry was more like a stalk of grass than a branch of the family tree. He was small for his age, and spindly. His hair, when it grew, was pale yellow and silky. Left to itself, it curled all over his head like a cherub's, but it was not left to itself for long. His father saw to that.

'For heaven's sake, Isobel, take that boy to have his hair cut. He looks just like a girl,' he would say, and if Mum told him that she was too busy, he took the little boy himself and had his hair cut so short that his head looked like a ping pong ball, and all his sisters laughed and called him a skinhead.

Harry cried.

His father did not shout at him. He took him on his lap and said very gravely, 'Boys don't cry, Harry. Remember. You can't learn that soon enough if you want to grow up into a big, strong man like me. Your cousin Marcus never cries. Try and be like him.'

'For heaven's sake, Victor,' Isobel said. 'He's only six, poor kid. I could cry myself. All those lovely curls gone. Where have you been all your life? Open your eyes next time you go out in the streets. Lots of young men have long curly hair. And very nice they look too.'

'Not my son,' Victor George Wellington said. 'I see I'll have to take him in hand.'

Harry ran upstairs to his room and shut the door behind him. He didn't want his father to take him in hand. It was not that he was frightened of his father; at least not very much. His father had never hit him. In fact it was his mother who occasionally slapped his legs when he had a tantrum, but she never hurt more than his dignity and he knew she loved him. He wasn't so certain about his father. He thought Dad tried to love him but never quite succeeded.

His door opened and he jumped.

'It's not Dad, it's me,' his sister Georgie said. 'Don't worry about him. He won't come. He's talking to Mum. Very seriously. What have you done now?'

'He's cross because I cried. He says boys don't cry, but I do. I can't help it. Tears just come out. I don't know how to stop them, Georgie. What can I do?'

Georgina smiled and hugged him. She was his favourite sister, a warm girl with soft brown eyes and freckles on her nose. 'You cry all you like, Harry. Dad's wrong. Boys do cry. And those who don't, should. Better than hitting people. Like Marcus does.'

'Does Dad hit people?' Harry asked nervously.

'No. No, he doesn't. He's not so bad, really, I suppose,' she added generously, 'but he's terribly old-fashioned. Mum says he's positively Victorian. And he expects too much. That's his trouble. Do you know what he said when I won my silver medal?'

'No. What?'

'He said, "Bad luck, Georgie. Never mind, you bring me back the gold next year." Bad luck! I'd been delighted with the silver. Ecstatic! When he said that, I could've thrown it at him.'

'I wish you had.'

There were footsteps on the stairs and his three other sisters came in.

'Oh, there you are,' Victoria said. 'You are a little mutt, Harry. Crying because you've lost a few curls! They'll grow again, silly. Now you've gone and put Dad in a bad mood for the rest of the day just when I wanted to borrow some money from him.'

'It wasn't because of my curls. I don't care about them.'

'Why was it, then?'

Harry couldn't explain. It had been the expression in his father's face when he'd seen the short hair. The pleased way he'd said, 'Ah, that's better. Now you look like a proper boy.' Harry knew what his father had meant by a proper boy. He meant a boy like Marcus, a boy who enjoyed riding tall horses with big yellow teeth. A boy who liked to play cricket with a hard ball that left bruises, and would sail with his father in a small boat on a rough, stomach-shaking sea, without being sick. Harry didn't think he could be that sort of boy. He didn't quite know what sort of boy he wanted to be, but he wished his dad would leave him to choose for himself.

'He says he can't help it,' Georgina told her sisters. 'He's only six. Didn't you ever cry when you were small, Vicky?'

'I don't think so. I don't remember,' Victoria replied. 'I think I was always tough.'

'I cried,' Julie said. 'I remember it well. My nose ran and Dad told me to wipe it. He said I looked disgusting with snot all over my face, so I decided to give up crying for ever.' She looked at herself in the mirror and smiled at her reflection. She was the prettiest of Harry's sisters, with hair as long and curly as his had been before it was cut.

'How?' he asked.

'How what? Oh, you mean, how did I stop myself crying? Let me see. I started by biting my lip, sometimes so hard it bled.'

'Didn't that make you cry more?'

'No. It sort of distracts your attention from what you were crying about. Then someone says, "Your lip's bleeding" and you say, "Oh is it really?" as if you hadn't noticed, and by the time you've finished talking about it, you've forgotten what you were crying about, see?'

'Mmmm,' Harry said doubtfully.

'Well, you try it,' Julie said kindly. 'I'll help you. And I'll teach you how to turn somersaults, if you like. Nothing like somersaults for cheering you up.

'I'll help you too,' Georgie offered. 'I'll teach you to

swim. In warm water,' she added, seeing he did not look any too pleased. 'It's lovely, honestly, Harry. And everyone has a wet face when they're swimming. Dad won't even notice if you cry.'

'And I'll lend you my gun,' said Nell, not to be outdone, though what she meant him to do with it, Harry wasn't sure. She was a silly girl.

'You're mad, all of you,' Victoria told her sisters. 'Somersaults and swimming and a gun! Supposing he wants to cry in the middle of the High Street? What's he to do then? All this fuss over Harry. Nobody bothered about us. We had to learn to swim at school, like everyone else. Nobody taught us to turn somersaults. We just copied the other kids. Dad was mean to us. He wouldn't even let me have riding lessons,' she added with an old bitterness, 'he said he couldn't afford it. But Harry! He can afford them for Harry. Harry can have everything he wants.'

'I don't want riding lessons. I don't think I like horses,' Harry explained.

'You're an idiot. You don't have to like them to sit on them,' Victoria told him scornfully. She turned to her sisters. 'You can't teach him anything. He's just a little coward. I'm not going to waste my time on him.'

Georgie told her she was mean, and Julie said it was just as well Vicky refused to help Harry, since she was a bully like Marcus, and would only make things worse. Nell said that Marcus had stepped on her china cat and broken it, and if Vicky broke anything of hers, she'd shoot her with her toy gun. They started quarrelling so loudly that Harry got into his bed, put his fingers in his ears, and waited for them to go away.

By the time they'd finished their quarrel, he was fast asleep. When they looked down at him, seeing his short, shaven head and the tear stains still streaking his flushed cheeks, even Victoria said softly, 'Poor little squirt,' and they agreed they would all help him and teach him what they could, and stop him being bullied at school.

Over the years Harry learned to hide his tears from his father. He learned to swim, though he never won any sort of medal. He rode an overlarge horse and fell off several times, breaking his collarbone twice and his arm once, and bit his lip till it bled but did not cry.

'Brave lad,' his father said, but added rather sadly, when Harry fell off once again, 'I don't think riding is your thing, is it, Harry? Perhaps we'd better give it up. I don't want you to break your neck. At least we tried.'

'The saddle is so slippery,' Harry apologised. 'Mum says I'd do better on a camel.'

'A camel?'

'She says they have cloth saddles like rugs, and a big

pommel in front to hold on to with both hands,' Harry explained.

'How on earth does she know?'

'She was a teacher once, Dad,' Harry said, surprised that his father seemed to have forgotten.

'I know that, you silly boy,' his father said impatiently, 'but I've never heard that they teach camel riding in English schools.' He looked sideways at his son and added, 'I could try and find out for you if you wish, but I don't think you'd like it, Harry. Camels are a lot higher off the ground than horses.'

Harry flushed, realising then that for all his and his sisters' efforts, his father still knew he was a coward. He felt almost sorry for him, having such a disappointing son.

'Vicky loves horses, Dad,' he said. 'And she's very brave. She can ride, you know. She's practised on her friends' pony. But it's too small for her really. I'm sure she'd love to have proper lessons.'

It was his father's turn to flush. 'Yes. Yes. She did say something about it once, years ago, but we were hard up then. I couldn't afford it. I suppose I should have thought of it later, but somehow . . . Well, she can have lessons instead of you, if she likes. Your mother can drive her over –'

'I think she'd rather you did, Dad.'

'Oh you do, do you? Has your sister put you up to this?'

'No, Dad!'

'If she really wants riding lessons, she'll accept a lift from me or your mother, just as it suits us. Or go by bus, if we're both too busy. And you can tell her that. The idea! Putting down conditions –'

'She didn't, Dad. She doesn't know anything about it. It was my idea.'

His father snorted but said no more until they got home. Then he said, 'You can tell Victoria to let me know when she can go for lessons and I'll fix it up with the stables.'

'Thank you, Dad.'

Victoria was delighted when he told her. 'But did he actually say he wanted me to come in your place or was that your idea? No, don't bother to lie. I can see from your face he didn't even think of me.'

She looked so cross that for a moment he was afraid she was going to swear and shout and refuse to have any lessons, but then she tossed her head. 'I don't care! Stupid old Dad, as long as he pays for my lessons, I'll take them and be glad.' She put her arm round Harry and hugged him. 'You're a good kid.'

Harry smiled.

Harry hated sailing. Georgie had taught him to swim but could not teach him how not to be seasick in a small boat. 'You'll get over it in time,' Dad said, but Harry did not.

Now the holidays had begun, and Vicky and Georgie were back home from college, his father was still determined to teach Harry to sail.

'You should take one of those pills I gave you,' he said impatiently the next time they were out on the choppy sea. 'You're beginning to look green again.'

'I tried one last week but it didn't work. In fact, it made me feel worse.'

His father was silent for a moment; then he said, 'Perhaps if I took you out for a long trip, a week or two, it might cure you once and for all.'

Harry didn't answer. He couldn't. He was hanging over the side of the boat being horribly sick. His father sighed, and pushing the tiller round, made for the shore. As they were walking home, he looked down at his son. The boy was not crying, but his face was as white as a cuttlefish. He looked utterly miserable.

'Oh, all right, Harry,' his father said with rough kindness, 'I won't take you out again. It obviously isn't your thing.'

'Sorry, Dad.'

'Not your fault.'

Harry glanced at his father. Perhaps this was the right time to ask. He opened his mouth . . .

'What is it, Harry?' his father asked. 'You look just like a fish. Speak up, boy, if there's something you want to say. Otherwise shut your mouth.'

'It's just . . . George would like to go sailing, Dad, and I'm sure she'd not be sick. She loves anything to do with water. Remember all those medals she's won for swimming in the county championships –'

'Yes, indeed. How many is it now? Five silvers and one bronze?'

'Not everyone can win the gold!' Harry said hotly.

'No, of course not.' His father sounded surprised, having forgotten the unlucky remark that had so offended Georgina in the past. 'Oh well. Tell Georgina she can come sailing with me instead of you.' He was silent for a moment. Then he looked down at Harry and added, 'You're quite clever in your way, aren't you, Harry? What about Julie? Are you going to tell me she's longing to play cricket with me? And Nell wants to come to football matches with me? And all the other things you do with me only because you're too frightened to refuse? Are you really so scared of me that you can't say straight out, "No thank you, Dad"?'

Harry flushed, the bright colour flooding his pale face. There were times when he almost hated his father.

'I'm not scared of you, Dad,' he said angrily. 'I'm sorry for you.'

'*You* are sorry for *me*?'

'Yes, I am,' Harry said, stung by the contempt in his father's voice.

'Do you mind telling me why?'

'Because you're never happy, that's why! You always want something you haven't got. Like a gold medal from Georgie when she's just won the silver. Like a boy from Mum when she's just given you a girl. Four girls! I bet every time you saw the next one, you didn't even smile. How do you think that made them feel? Didn't you care? And then when you have a son at last, it isn't the right sort. Oh no, you wanted a son like Marcus. But all you got was me. Tough luck.'

His father's face was as red as fire, but when he spoke, his voice was cold. 'Have you quite finished, Harry?'

Might as well be hung for a sheep as a lamb, Harry thought.

'No. I want to say I'm sorry for Uncle William, too.'

'And what has he done to displease you?'

'He had a son like Marcus, that's what. How you can prefer him to me, I don't know. It's – it's an insult!' Harry shouted. 'I wouldn't have minded so much if he'd been a decent sort of boy, but he's not. He's horrible!'

For a long time his father did not say anything. His mouth was tightly shut as if he was afraid to open it in case he exploded.

I've done it now, thought Harry.

They walked towards the car park in silence. For all its disadvantages, Harry was used to being his father's favourite child. It made a special bond between them, even though at times the bond was more like a chain.

At last, his father said quietly, 'Try not to be envious of your cousin just because he is more successful than you.'

'Not at everything! Only at sport and not even all sports, either. I can run faster than he can. Much faster.'

'I expect you've had a lot of practice running away,' his father said.

Later, when they were driving home, he apologised as he usually did when he thought he'd hurt Harry's feelings. 'I'm sorry. That was an unkind thing to say. It's not your fault. I know you try hard. Don't think I haven't noticed.'

Harry did not answer.

The next morning was warm and sunny. He found three of his sisters in the garden. Georgie was painting her toenails green to match the grass. Victoria was sitting on a wooden chair, shelling some broad beans for their mother, and Julie was standing on her head, showing off. Nell was spending the day with a school friend.

'Hullo, Harry,' Georgie said. 'Are you at a loose end, too? It's only the third week of our holidays and I've nothing better to do than paint my toenails. Do you like them?'

'Yes, but you should have painted them sea-green, not

grass-green,' he said. 'Dad wants you to go sailing with him on Saturday. He asked me to tell you.'

'What? But he's always said that the boat won't hold more than two.'

'I won't be going.'

Julie came down from her headstand and sat cross-legged on the grass. They all stared at him.

'Something's happened, hasn't it?' Georgie said. 'I thought you looked a bit off colour last night. Have you had a row with Dad?'

'I was sick again. I'm sure he thinks I do it to annoy him.'

'He can't really. If he said so, it was probably his idea of a joke,' Victoria said. 'You know how clumsy he can be, always offending people. But he can be jolly nice when you get to know him. Since I've been riding with him, I've got to like him a lot. He's really quite different . . . You go sailing with him, Georgie.'

'I don't think I'd better. I might be tempted to push him overboard.'

Harry knew she really wanted to go, and said quickly, 'No, you won't. You'll enjoy it. And I'll try and think of something for Julie –'

'Don't bother!' Julie cried. 'I'm not doing anything boring just to get to know Dad better. Besides, I already get on quite well with him as it is.'

'That's because you're his idea of a proper girl,' Harry said. 'You're pretty and fluffy –'

'And vain,' said Georgie.

'And silly,' Vicky added.

'And you're all just jealous,' Julie said, not in the least put out by this. 'You know, Dad thinks gymnastics are like dancing lessons for little girls. He's no idea what a hard discipline it is.'

'Why don't you invite him to see your next show at school?' Harry suggested.

'He wouldn't come. He'd find something to be too busy with. You know what's he's like.'

'I think I can get him to come,' Victoria said slowly. 'He's changing a bit. He listens more. He's nicer. What have you been doing to him, Harry?'

'Educating Dad, that's my plan,' Harry said, and laughed. 'I'm trying to teach him to appreciate his daughters. I've given up trying to teach him to appreciate his son.'

'Harry! Don't say that!'

'It's all right. I feel wonderful! I feel free! I'm not going to try and be what Dad wants any longer. I'm not going to go into the boring family business when I leave school. A chain of butchers' shops – can you see me going round the country counting sausages? I'm practically a vegetarian. From now on, I'm going to be me and do what suits me.'

'And what's that?' they asked.

'I don't know,' he said and laughed with them. 'Isn't it wonderful?' He flung his arms up into the sunny air. 'I can be anything. Anything at all. I feel like turning cartwheels and somersaults in the air! I'm free as a bird!'

Harry had grown into a tall, amiable boy, and was well-liked at school. He knew his mother and his sisters loved him, and for a while he thought that was enough. He was a member of the Riverside Harriers and ran for his school. He had learned to play the trumpet and sing the latest songs. He could speak French and Italian fairly well and was going on a walking tour on the continent with his friends next year.

And yet there was a hole in his life, an empty space around the edges of which his father walked politely, like a stern, silent ghost. Never shouting, never losing his temper, never asking for his company.

'How is he?' Harry sometimes asked his sisters, who knew Dad better now than he did.

'He's fine,' they said, and they added, looking at him sideways, 'but he misses you.'

'Oh yeah? Why doesn't he ask me out somewhere then?'

'You know how proud he is. He'd be afraid of losing face –'

What about my face? Harry thought. But his face was young, he could afford to lose a bit of it here and there. It would grow again.

But did he really want to put himself back into bondage to his father, now that he was free? Oddly enough, the answer was yes. He too had changed. He was old enough and strong enough to resist the weight of his father's ambitions for him, and go his own way. All his life Harry had wanted his father to admire him. It was a dream he couldn't give up. So when the local teams started playing football again in the park, he asked his father if he'd like to come and watch.

At first he thought his father was not going to answer. But then he said, 'I thought you didn't like watching football with me, Harry.'

'That was cricket. I do like football.'

'Then let's go,' said his father, smiling at him. 'By all means, let's go.'

They went nearly every week and enjoyed themselves. One day his father asked Harry to come to the Cup Final with him. 'I have two tickets,' he told him, smiling.

Harry was surprised. 'But, Dad, don't you usually take Marcus?'

'That boy!' his father said, in a tone of voice that made Harry's heart sing. 'I've been gravely disappointed in your cousin Marcus. I've been hearing things about him, very unpleasant things . . . Not that I'd believe mere gossip, of course, but it made me watch him carefully myself. I tell you, Harry, that boy's a lout and a bully. I saw him with my own eyes twist your sister Nell's arm, and laugh when she cried! And when I told him what I thought of him, he refused to apologise. He called me an old – well, never mind what he said. I never thought to hear such language from him. I'm sorry for my poor brother having such a son. You were right. You never liked him, did you?'

'No,' Harry agreed happily.

'I find that neither your mother nor your sisters liked him either; I was the only one who was blind. However, my eyes are open now. You are the boy a father can be proud of. Not Marcus, but you.'

Sad Ada

There's some sort of mystery about my aunt Ada. I don't know what it is. She is nice to me and always brings me presents when we meet.

'You'll spoil her,' my mother used to say uneasily. She was always uneasy when Ada came. I had a feeling she didn't like her hugging and kissing me, though I couldn't think why. She was normally pleased when people made a fuss of me, so long as they didn't give me too many sweets. Aunt Ada didn't give me too many sweets, she just gave me too many kisses. She was very pale and thin. Perhaps she was ill and Mum was afraid of my catching something.

But when I asked my mother, she said quickly, 'No, of course not. Whatever gave you that idea?'

'You did,' I said, but I couldn't explain why, so I turned away and started playing with my jigsaw as if I'd forgotten all about Aunt Ada.

'Children notice things,' Emmie said to Mum in a very low voice. They have been friends since childhood and tell each other all the secrets they don't tell me. I hoped if I went on playing with my jigsaw and looking as deaf as I could, I'd find out Aunt Ada's secret.

'It's just that I can't relax when Ada's here,' my mother murmured to Emmie.

'Surely you don't think she would – 'Emmie began. Then she stopped. 'Somebody's got big ears,' she said, by which she meant me, though my name isn't somebody, it's Cecily, and my ears are a perfectly normal size.

'Would what?' I asked, giving up my pretence of being deaf.

'Wouldn't forget to post my letter,' Emmie said promptly. I thought she was lying. She always speaks quickly when she's telling a lie so as not to give you time to think. 'Whenever I give someone a letter to post,' she went on, 'I spend the rest of the week wondering if it's still in their pocket, down among the old bus tickets and dirty hankies.'

My mother smiled but shook her head. 'Ada never puts anything in her pockets. She says it makes them baggy and shapeless. Like mine.' She sighed, looking down at her shabby old cardigan. 'Ada is always so beautifully dressed.'

'She must spend a fortune on her clothes,' Emmie said

enviously, 'a positive fortune. Oh well, we can't all be rich.'

'Money hasn't made her happy. I wouldn't like to have her dreams at night –' Mum broke off, remembering me.

'Why not? What does she dream of?' I asked.

'Nothing,' my mother said. 'Nothing to do with you.'

'Mind your own business,' Emmie told me. She is very rude. I hoped Ada had stolen her letter.

Stolen! *Was that it*? Was Aunt Ada a thief.

Was that why Mum was uneasy whenever Ada came? Whenever Aunt Ada hugged me, her long fair hair falling over me like a silken shawl, perhaps Mum thought she was trying to steal the thin silver chain I wore round my neck, the one Dad had given me.

I didn't tell them that I'd guessed. I knew it was a really bad secret and I mustn't talk about it, not to anyone. Aunt Ada was Dad's sister. He wouldn't like it if she went to prison.

Every time now that Aunt Ada came to visit, I hid my silver chain under my mattress. When she gave me presents, I wondered if she'd paid for them. I set her tests. I'd leave fifty pence on the coffee table while I went to help Mum in the kitchen. But when I came back, the money was always still there.

For all my watching, I never saw her steal anything, but I began to notice other things about her. How sad she looked. Her eyes were as grey and shiny as a rainy day. Her mouth drooped at the corners, and sometimes when she put her thin hand up to cover it, her fingers trembled so much that the diamonds seemed to dance in her rings.

One day I saw her eyes brim with tears. 'Are you going to cry, Aunt Ada?' I asked in dismay. I was older now and not so shy.

She shook her head and went and stood looking out of the window so I couldn't see her face any longer. Then she said, turning round and smiling at me, 'No, I don't think so, darling. I hope not. I do cry sometimes, don't you?'

'Yes.'

'When did you cry last?' she asked, just for something to say.

'The day before yesterday. I hurt my head. At least, I didn't hurt it. Bertie did. He's the boy next door. He's got a terrible temper. He threw a stick at me just because I said he was stupid. It bled and bled –' I broke off because Aunt Ada had gone so pale I thought she was going to faint.

'It's all right,' I reassured her, 'Mum bathed it with T.C.P. and put a plaster on.' I pushed my fringe back to show her the tiny plaster. 'It wasn't really such a very big stick,' I admitted, 'it just felt like it. Bertie howled even louder than I did.'

'I expect he was frightened when he saw the blood.'

'No. It was because I kicked his ankle. Hard,' I said with satisfaction.

'Cecily!'

'Well, the stick hurt me. He deserved it. Don't you think he deserved it?'

She did not answer, but turned her face away. I felt she disapproved of me.

'I didn't tell his Mum or Dad. I didn't sneak on him. That was good of me, wasn't it?' I said.

'I don't know. Perhaps if we do wrong, we ought to be punished. Perhaps if we aren't, we feel sad about it for the rest of our life.'

I stared at her. I didn't think she was talking about Bertie any more. Or me. I thought she was talking about herself. Was it being a thief that gave her bad dreams and made her cry? Or something worse?

The next day, I went to play with Bertie. He is my friend when he's not being horrid. We are both only children, and need someone nearby to talk to.

We sat on the grass, eating apples.

'My aunt Ada thinks you should've been punished for

throwing the stick at me,' I informed Bertie. 'She thinks I should tell on you.'

'Your aunt Ada is a mad cat,' he said. 'Everybody knows that. Except you. I bet you don't know what she gets up to.'

'Oh, yes I do,' I boasted, annoyed at his smug expression, 'I found out ages ago.'

'You never told me!'

'Why should I? It's a secret. You can't expect me to sneak on my aunt.'

'A secret!' he said laughing. 'What secret? There isn't any gossip about her, silly. I made it up. She's just a boring old aunt like anybody else's.'

'She's not! She's a thief!' I cried.

I was sorry the moment I said it, but it was too late. 'She's not really,' I went on quickly, 'That's just what Mum's stupid friend Emmie thinks. She gave Aunt Ada a letter to post and now she's going round saying Aunt Ada stole it. Well, not saying it exactly. Sort of hinting.'

'Why would anyone want to steal a letter?'

I didn't answer.

'Perhaps it had money in it,' Bertie said hopefully. 'It might have been stuffed with ten pound notes that crackled when she touched it. Perhaps your auntie's a well known thief and has stolen lots of things before. I wouldn't be surprised. She has a sort of slippery look.'

'Shut up, Bertie! Aunt Ada's nice. I like her. She gives me lots of presents –'

'She does, does she? You want to be careful, Cessie,' he told me, trying not to laugh, 'don't let the neighbours see them. You could get into trouble, you know. Receiver of stolen teddy bears.'

I couldn't help smiling, and soon we were both laughing and I was telling him about my trying to trap Aunt Ada with my pocket money. But I made him promise not to tell anyone, cross his heart and hope to die.

Two weeks later, I saw my mother and Bertie's mother, Flora, talking over the garden fence. My mum looked flushed and angry, and Flora's voice was shrill. I thought they were quarrelling at first, but they weren't. They were agreeing with each other.

Mum was saying, 'Nonsense. It's absolute nonsense.'

'That's what I told them,' Flora said. 'I told them to their faces that I didn't believe a word of it, but it was no good. They said everybody knew. I wasn't going to tell you at first, dear, but, well, I thought perhaps you'd want to know.'

'Did you really? I suppose I ought to thank you,' Mum said, not sounding at all grateful. 'Though what I can do about it, I can't think. It's too absurd. Ada a thief, of all people! Ada's a director of Bennington Worldwide

Chemicals. She earns more money than we do, and only has herself to spend it on. She doesn't need to steal. If I find out who started this stupid rumour –'

She saw me and stopped. Stared.

'Oh, it's you, Cecily,' she said slowly, 'I wish you wouldn't creep about so. What do you want?'

'I was looking for Bertie.'

'He's in the kitchen, making us some sandwiches,' Flora told me. 'You're coming to tea with us, had you forgotten? Why don't you go and help him, Cecily? Otherwise he'll eat them all himself and leave none for us.'

I was glad to get away. I didn't like the distrustful look on my mother's face so I went to the kitchen and found Bertie cutting up tomatoes. Bertie the sneak. Bertie who must have told.

'It wasn't me!' he protested, warding off the blow I was aiming at him. 'I swear it. God's truth!'

'I told nobody but you! So who else could it have been?'

'What about Emmie? She's probably told hundreds of people.'

I didn't answer. I was trying to remember what Emmie had actually said. Maybe she hadn't mentioned the word 'thief', but what else was I to think?

'Poor Aunt Ada,' I said. 'They won't ask her to their

parties any more. They'll cut her dead in the street. It'll be the last straw. She'll probably kill herself.' My voice shook. I could almost see her hanging from a tree by the river, her long hair covering her face.

'No, she won't. Cheer up, Cessie.' Bertie put his arm round me and kissed my cheek. He can be very sweet when he wants. 'Mum's friends are ghastly. Your aunt will be glad to be rid of them. Nobody could enjoy their parties. Tell you what, I'll ask your aunt to my birthday party, and we'll drink her health in champagne.'

I'd been to some of Bertie's parties and they were terrible.

'Aunt Ada's too old for your sort of party,' I said.

'Perhaps you're right. Don't worry, Cessie. I'll think of something else. Bound to, if I put my mind to it.'

I couldn't resist reminding him how often his ideas had led to disaster in the past. He picked up a tomato to throw at me, then changed his mind and ate it instead.

The door opened and our mothers came in to inquire after the sandwiches.

'We're starving,' Flora complained. 'What have you been doing all this time?'

'Talking.'

'What about?'

'Aunt Ada,' I said. 'We've heard the rumours about her.'

'You shouldn't listen to rumours,' Flora said, and my mother frowned at me. She did not say anything, however, and by the time we'd settled down to tea and sandwiches, seemed to have forgotten what I'd said. They started talking about gardening, ignoring us.

Bertie sidled up to me. 'Why did you mention the rumours?' he whispered.

'I'm going to have it out with Mum when we get home. I'm sick of secrets.'

'Can I come?'

'No. Mum won't tell me anything if you're there. She'd just clam up.'

'I suppose so,' he admitted, then added, 'if she does tell you, you must tell me afterwards everything she says. Every word.'

'Why should I tell you my family secrets?'

'Because I'm your friend,' he said hopefully.

When we got home, Mum went into the sitting-room and switched on the television. I switched it off again, and told her I wanted to talk.

'Please, Mum. It's important.'

She sighed, but sat down on the sofa, patting the seat beside her. 'Come and sit down. Now, what's more important than the News?'

'I want you to tell me about Aunt Ada.'

'There's been too much talk about her already,' she said sharply. 'I hope it wasn't you and Bertie who've been spreading these stupid rumours around –'

'No, it wasn't! Why do you always suspect us? It was Emmie saying that Aunt Ada stole her letter –'

'Stole her letter?' Then she remembered. 'Cessie, she was joking. You don't understand –'

'How can I? You never tell me anything. If I guess wrong, it's your fault. You and Emmie whispering your secrets . . . I'm not stupid. Even when I was small, I knew you didn't like Aunt Ada coming here. When she hugged me, I could see you wanted to snatch me away from her. Why? She's your sister-in-law. Even if she is a thief, even if she's been to prison, you ought to . . . to protect her, not betray her . . .'

'Cessie, calm down.' My mother put her arm round me and shook me gently. 'I wouldn't betray Ada. Don't be so melodramatic. It's just – oh, I don't want to talk about it. It happened a long time ago, when we were children. I want to forget those days.'

'Did it happen in Framlington?' I asked.

Framlington was the village where Mum had lived when she was twelve, in a big manor house divided into flats. It was here that Mum had first met Dad, who was also twelve. They were all there, Emmie and her brother Pete in the flat on one side, Dad and Ada in the flat on the other. And on the top floor, a couple with a little girl called Fay.

I thought it sounded romantic; the big garden where the children all played, a garden with trees to climb, shrubs to hide behind and a big lawn for their ball games. There was even a small shallow pond with newts and frogs and rushes; and a hammock swung between two trees.

But I had noticed that Mum did not like talking about it much. Once when I'd said it must have been wonderful, her face became shadowed and she gave a little shiver and looked quite ill. But she would not tell me what the matter was. Now I wondered if Ada was the cause.

'Was it in Framlington that Ada started stealing?' I asked. 'Did Emmie see her do it? Did Ada go to prison?'

'No, no! Ada's not a thief.'

'What is she, then?'

'Unlucky,' my mother said, and for an awful moment I thought she was going to cry.

'Mum!'

'Oh, Cessie, we used to call her the jinx. Just teasing, you know. Poor Ada. Everything went wrong for her. Little things at first. Her pet rabbit died. One of the dogs chewed up her favourite doll. She lost her bracelet, she dropped her expensive camera in the pond. If you lent her something, she'd lose it or break it, and then cry. Nobody wanted to play with her.

'Mum, it wasn't her fault.'

'I know. You're right, of course, but – but it wasn't really our fault either. She was too young for us, that was the trouble. She was only seven. She didn't like doing the things we did. Climbing trees and playing with the dogs. She was even frightened of the cows in the field, and always wanted to be carried across. At first, we'd take turns, but she was quite heavy in spite of being so thin. In the end we'd laugh and run on and leave her behind. And we were glad. We didn't want her with us, in case her bad luck rubbed off on to us. "Go home, Jinx!" we'd shout.'

'You left her alone,' I said reproachfully, 'so that whatever was going to happen could happen to her and not you. I think that's dreadful.'

For a moment my mother did not say anything. I thought she looked pale and guilty. When she went on, she spoke in a low voice, not looking at me.

'We didn't leave her alone, of course we didn't. There was always one of the mothers there. They arranged it between them, taking it in turns. When Fay and her family came to live in the top flat, Ada became very friendly with them. She liked helping Mrs Allen look after the little girl, who was only two. "Fairy" she called her, because she was so small and pretty.

'One day, when I was hurrying to catch up the others,

I found Ada wheeling Fairy round the garden in her buggy, bumping her over the grass and both of them screaming with laughter.

'It made me uneasy to see them. There were dark clouds blocking out the sun, although it was still hot. In the distance I could hear the others calling me, "Kitty! Kitty! Kitty!"

'"They're calling you," Ada had said. "You'd better hurry up or you'll miss the bus."

'"Are you on your own? Where's Mrs Allen?"

'"In her flat. Up there, keeping an eye on us. Not that she needs to. I can manage by myself. I've done it before. Go on, Kitty, go away! We don't want Kitty, do we, Fairy?"

'The little girl had smiled at me, and said, "Yeth, we do. Kitty. Kitty cat. Me want Kitty."

'"But not as much as you want me. You love me best, don't you, Fairy?" Ada asked. It mattered to her. She had been snubbed too often. She needed to be loved.

'But Fairy giggled, and began chanting, "Me love Kitty best! Kitty best!" And I laughed. It was so silly. She hardly knew me; it was the name she liked.

'Ada was furiously hurt.

'"Well, you can have her then!" she cried, and pushed the buggy violently across the grass.

'I suppose she aimed it at me. It may have been the

grass that deflected it and made it swerve away from me on to a steep concrete path, where it quickly gathered speed. I ran after it but, before I could reach it, it crashed into a large rockery at the next bend and overturned, landing upside down on the rocks. There was no sign of Fairy. When I righted the buggy, I saw she was still strapped in, lying with her eyes shut and her face horribly covered with blood.'

My mother stopped and caught her breath. 'I shouldn't be telling you this,' she said.

I took her hand and held it tight. 'Was she dead?'

'No, not dead. But her face – she must have smashed it on a sharp rock. It was terribly scarred and she lost one of her eyes. Poor child. Though the surgeons patched her up, Fairy never looked the same again, and she used to be so pretty. Ada blamed herself, of course. She was quite ill with guilt, although Mrs Allen was very good. She told Ada it wasn't her fault, it was just a terrible accident.

'Ada's sensitive, though. When Mrs Allen told her Fairy was not allowed visitors, she knew that Mrs Allen could not forgive her. "They never want to see me again," she said. "They can't bear the sight of me. They didn't say so exactly but it's true. They're moving house, you know. I've asked her for their new address but she always makes some excuse . . . So I'll never see Fairy again. I'll never be able to say sorry."

'We tried to comfort her. We made a point of always asking her to come out with us, even though we secretly longed for her to say no. We were much kinder. But I've never really felt at ease with her to this day, even though she's now my sister-in-law. I can't forget the expression on her face when she pushed the buggy.'

'What do you mean?'

'I don't know, Cessie. She looked – spiteful. Vicious. I felt I could never trust her again. And then when you were a baby, you looked so like Fairy. I'm sure you reminded Ada of her. She was always hugging and kissing you, like she used to hug and kiss Fairy. It frightened me. I wanted to say, "Go away, Jinx! Don't touch my baby!" But how could I? She's your dad's sister and he's fond of her.'

Mum sighed, and added, 'So now you know what happened. Remember it was an accident, Cessie. I mustn't be unjust. It was nobody's fault.'

I didn't agree with her. I thought it was everybody's fault. Poor sad Ada. And poor Mum, too.

I told Bertie everything. I know I'd promised my mother not to, but I had to tell someone. I felt so muddled. I'd loved my aunt but I couldn't forget what my mother had said about never trusting her again.

'I keep looking at Ada's face, expecting it to change into something nasty,' I told him.

'Come off it, Cessie,' Bertie said. 'She was only seven, you said. Look at me. I'm thirteen and I threw that stick at you. Didn't mean to hurt you, just lost my temper. Supposing I'd hit you in the eye and blinded you? Would that have made me a monster?'

'Yes,' I said decidedly.

'*Cessie*! Mind you, I felt like a monster when I saw the blood. I haven't thrown anything at you since then, have I? Or anyone else, come to that. And I don't suppose your aunt has pushed any more babies into a rockery. People change. She doesn't look vicious to me. She looks sad and soppy, as if she's about to burst into tears at any minute. You ought to do something about it.'

'Me? What can I do?'

'I don't know. Why don't you ask your dad? She's his sister.'

So I did. Dad knew that Mum had told me about the accident, but all he said was, 'I hope you'll be a good girl, Cessie, and not chatter about it. Ada's unhappy enough as it is. We don't want to keep reminding her.'

'I don't think she can forget, Dad. Bertie thinks it might help if she could see Fairy again to say sorry. If Fairy forgave her and said she was quite happy, it might take away Aunt Ada's sadness.'

'Supposing Fairy isn't happy? Supposing she's miserable and won't forgive her?' Dad asked.

'Bertie said we could visit her first and find out. If Fairy won't forgive her, we wouldn't have to tell Ada anything. But we don't know Fairy's address.'

'I do, as it happens,' my father said. 'You'd better leave it to me.'

When Dad came back, he told me that Fay was married and fat, and perfectly happy to see Ada. She no longer looked like a fairy, she looked more like an apple dumpling. The scars hardly showed on her face and she had a china eye. 'Or plastic,' he said, 'I couldn't tell which. I didn't like to stare.'

She lived in Cornwall, had three sons and a doctor husband, and bred poodles. When Dad and Ada drove down to see her, she kissed Ada and gave her a little apricot poodle puppy.

'It was very kind of her,' Aunt Ada told me, 'especially as she didn't remember me. I had to tell her who I was. Then she laughed and said of course she'd forgiven me, it was all so long ago, she couldn't remember a thing about it. She gave me this puppy. It keeps biting my fingers.'

'Don't you like it?' I asked. 'I'll have it if you don't want it.'

She shook her head. 'No, I shall keep it for ever, as a penance,' she said, 'and I'll call it Clem. Short for Clemency.'

'Don't you mean Clementine?'

'No. That's a small orange.' She looked down at the puppy and smiled. 'Clemency means mildness and mercy. I thought if I called it that, it might stop biting me.'

I think she likes Clem really. She seems much happier now.

Also by Vivien Alcock

The Cuckoo Sister

The owls were still hooting when I went back to bed, but they were not the birds in my mind. I was thinking about cuckoos. The cuckoo lays her egg in another bird's nest and flies away. And when the egg hatches, the young cuckoo grows bigger and bigger, until one day it pushes the true fledgling right out of the nest.

Kate's sister, Emma, was snatched from her pram as a baby and her parents have long since given up hope of finding their kidnapped child. But, thirteen years after Emma's disappearance, Rosie suddenly turns up on the doorstep with a letter claiming that she is the missing child. But is she? And can the family cope with this new addition?

Runner-up for the Young Observer Award.

'a deft psychological thriller . . .'
Books for Keeps

Also by *Vivien Alcock*

The Face at the Window

Nominated for the Carnegie Medal.

It was there again, watching me. Before it moved, I'd thought it was a mask, put there by one of the Harwoods to pay me out for having watched them.

When Lesley comes to stay with her aunt while her mother goes abroad to work, she has little else to do except watch. The Harwood children are older and seem superior – Lesley thinks it's a wonder they manage to have tea with her just once, their lives are so busy and full of good works.

But when Lesley asks about the child they're hiding, she realises the Harwoods aren't as superior as they seem and that they have problems of their own . . .

Also by Vivien Alcock

Ghostly Companions

It was the last straw. Furiously, he reached out and snatched off her mask.

'Oh God!' he screamed.

But what was it that he saw?

A collection of ten ghost stories written with Vivien Alcock's superb skill in blending the natural and the supernatural. A figurehead that is more than it seems, a patchwork made like none other, a mirror image that never leaves you alone, a garden that no child should enter at night, a masquerade that gives you the chance to be someone else . . . The settings vary from the familiar local Common to the exotic atmosphere of Venice while the moods vary from the funny to the frightening. A feast to satisfy all tastes by a master storyteller.

Also by Vivien Alcock

The Haunting of Cassie Palmer

'You believe in spirits yourself! I know you do!'

'Not any more I don't.'

'All right then Cassie Palmer, prove it. You're the gifted one. Let's see what you can do, O seventh child of a seventh child! Nothing to be scared of if you don't believe in it. And if it doesn't work, you'll know you're normal like us. '

Taunted and angry, Cassie calls to the spirits and an angry and fearsome spirit responds. Deverill stands before her at the gravestone – the haunting has begun . . .

Also by Vivien Alcock

A Kind of Thief

'Someone's got to look after the three of us.'

Elinor has always been seen as the strong one of the family. When her father is arrested, her stepmother can't cope and thirteen-year-old Elinor is left to look after the family. But at the time of his arrest, Elinor's father gives her the means to retrieve his case – which Elinor believes must be full of money.

Then, the children are sent off to different homes. Elinor takes the case with her but Timon, who also lives in Elinor's new home, makes her realise that she too is a kind of thief . . .

'Convincing storytelling rich with atmospheric imagery . . .'
The Guardian

Also by Vivien Alcock

The Monster Garden

'I shouldn't have done it. I didn't really mean to, but that's no excuse, of course. I should have known better with a name like mine. Frances Stein. Called Frankie for short. You can't really blame me for making a monster . . .'

The day she acquired some living tissue from the genetic engineering laboratory was the day Frankie's life changed for ever. She'd never imagined her experiment would be so successful, but how will she keep the growing monster a secret from her family?

The Monster Garden was shortlisted for the Smarties, Whitbread, Guardian and Federation of Children's Book Groups Awards, and was commended for the Carnegie Medal.

'this unusual and superbly imaginative novel is a triumph of story-telling.'
Times Educational Supplement

Also by Vivien Alcock

Singer to the Sea God

Beside the gilded chair, Cleo stood quietly, still holding in her hands the silver jug. Her hair, her skin were pale as white marble, delicately veined with grey at wrist and throat. Her clothes were of a darker grey and more porous substance and the silver jug was blackened where her fingers held it. It was as if whatever malignant force had struck her had, like lightning, passed right through her to alter everything she touched.

When Cleo is turned to stone after the return of Perseus, Phaidon feels he cannot leave her behind when he flees with his uncle and two other slaves. But the sea trader who has helped Phaidon and his friends now abandons them, taking Cleo with him. Marooned on an island haunted by strange echoes, they meet Iris, orphaned, friendless and longing to get to the mainland – but the mainland is six deaths away . . .

'a fine and absorbing novel. Vivien Alcock knows how to increase the tension almost to breaking point . . .'
Junior Bookshelf

Also by Vivien Alcock

The Stonewalkers

'Poppy, dear girl, she told herself, shutting her eyes tight and beginning to tremble, you may be the biggest liar out of hell, but you're not so far round the bend that you can't see both ways.'

Poppy isn't mad – the statue Belladonna really has come to life with the lightning flash. But Poppy Brown *is* a liar – so who will believe such things could happen – and worse, that the statue is a vengeful, furious creature, not the smiling friend Poppy once thought her?

A brilliant and chilling story.

***Also by* Vivien Alcock**

The Sylvia Game

Emily's relationship with her father, an unsuccessful artist, is tinged with mistrust since the bailiffs visited the family home. When he takes her on holiday to Devon and goes out on 'business' for a day, Emily therefore decides to follow him.

Losing the trail at the entrance to an old stately house, Emily comes into contact with Oliver – and discovers a connection between herself, her father and the mysterious Sylvia Game . . .

Also by Vivien Alcock

Time Wreck

'Spooky-Loonie,

Mary Frewin,

Tell us what your ghosts are doing . . .'

Mary wants somebody to believe her. She longs for somebody, *anybody,* to see one of her ghosts. Will Mary find the answer in her terrifying journey into another world?

Also by Vivien Alcock

The Trial of Anna Cotman

'There's a time to break promises and a time to keep them.'

When Anna Cotman arrives, bossy Lindy Miller appoints her as best friend. Anna, eager to please, joins the Society of Masks, swearing her allegiance in a chilling oath. Originally set up to combat bullying, the Som is now used by the older boys to bully and rule the younger ones. When Anna challenges their rules the leaders of the Som decide to discipline her. Anna is assigned a Defender and the terrifying countdown to her trial begins . . .

A stunning novel, shortlisted for the Carnegie Medal.